The Journey to Redemption

Twizz J.

This is a work of fiction. Names, characters, places and incidents either are products of the author's imagination or are used fictitiously. Any resemblance to actual events or locales or persons, living or dead, is entirely coincidental.

ISBN: 9798836531539

DEDICATION

I would like to dedicate this book to two important people.

The first one is my mom. Without you and your ways, not only would I not be living, but I would not have discovered a way out of the insanity I called life. Thank you, from now until eternity I will always look at Red Passion Alizé and smile. R.I.P beautiful.

And the second person who is the greatest of all. Son, without you coming about I don't think I would have slowed down for anything or anyone. Thanks for opening my eyes. And remember son, sometimes the things we don't feel comfortable doing become the things that change our lives for the better. Love you cuz.

CONTENTS

CHAPTER 1

"Good morning babies," DeCarlos greets his girlfriend Sarah and his unborn child.

He began to smile as he watched Sarah's eyes slowly open from her deep sleep as he stood over top of her. Sarah had emerald green eyes that sparkled when the sun from the bedroom window shined on them.

DeCarlos and Sarah were about to be young parents. Even though they were both seventeen years old, they have known each other for their entire lives. As kids on the playground, they made a pinky swear that they would remain friends for life--no matter what happens or where they might be.

"Good morning baby." Sarah responded after her eyes adjusted to the sunlight that was coming in from the curtain-drawn windows. As DeCarlos bent down to get closer to Sarah she reached up and wrapped her arms around his neck and gave him a kiss.

Sarah then noticed that DeCarlos had a tray in his hands with a plate on it that was piled up high with pancakes, sausage, bacon and scrambled eggs with cheese.

"Is that for me?" Sarah asked.

"No, it is not for you it's for DeCarlos Jr., you just get it by default." DeCarlos replied.

"Well give it here then, your son is absolutely starving this morning." Sarah sat up in bed and DeCarlos smiled as he gladly handed over the food tray.

DeCarlos walked around the bed and sat next to Sarah. He watched quietly as Sarah ate her bacon and pancakes first. He noticed her humming and dancing while she ate. The sight of this made him laugh a little.

"The bacon and pancakes must be good because you're dancing like you hear go-go music playing while you're eating again."

That made Sarah laugh. She knew DeCarlos was right on the money with his slick comment. After all, the pancakes were undeniably good. Sarah liked the fact that DeCarlos paid attention to her. She leaned over and gave DeCarlos a kiss.

"You know me so well."

"It's easy to know you when you chew like a horse and dance like Hammer" DeCarlos said, smiling all the while.

"Shut up boy" Sarah quickly said followed with a playful jab to DeCarlos' shoulder.

"Who made this anyway I know it wasn't you. You couldn't cook this good if your life depended on it."

DeCarlos got up and turned to Sarah.

"Oh, you trying to go on my cooking this early in the morning. Girl I can cook so good it will make you want to do the stanky leg"

DeCarlos showed Sarah how the stanky leg was done. And Sarah waved him off with a quick hand gesture.

"Boy who you playing with. I have been living here for five months and I have not once tasted any cooking from you that was anywhere as good as this. Seriously, who cooked this?" She asked again.

"You better be glad that I have to go to school cause I would go downstairs and cook you something so good you will end up delivering DeCarlos Jr a lot faster than you think."

"Boy whatever. You still ain't answer my question who cooked this" Sarah said pointing her fork at the pile of pancakes.

"Ma cooked it before she left to go to work," DeCarlos said with a smile on his face.

He went to the bedroom closet to grab his book bag. Watching DeCarlos get up and walk away made Sarah feel like she was going to be alone.

"DeCarlos, you know I love you right?"

"Yeah, I know, I love you too baby."

DeCarlos could hear something in her voice that didn't sit right with him.

"Sarah, what's wrong? DeCarlos looked at his watch.

"I have twenty-five minutes before school starts, so talk to me" DeCarlos sat next to Sarah on the bed.

"Well baby, I didn't think your parents would be cool with me staying here and them allowing me to stay here has brought me even closer to you and it has let me see the softer side of you."

DeCarlos gets up, grabs his jacket from off the hanger and thinks about what he was going to say for a second. Then it came to him.

"Sarah when your parents kicked you out for being pregnant my parents had no choice but to take you in, they're trying to teach me a lesson. Slowly but surely, I'm learning it. They teaching me responsibility and how to be caring. So, if you can see those qualities showing in my character then I guess the lesson they are trying to teach is working.

DeCarlos takes another glance at his watch and realizes that he has to hurry up.

"Baby, I have to hurry up before I'm late." He walks over to Sarah and gave her a kiss on the forehead then he looks her in the eyes.

"I love you Sarah"

"I love you too DeCarlos"

DeCarlos turns and heads out the door and down the steps. As he reaches for the doorknob on the front door his cell phone rings.

[Ring, Ring, Ring]

DeCarlos looks at the Caller ID on his phone and it reads Mom, so he picks up.

"Hello"

"Good morning DeCarlos."

"Good morning, Ma."

"Did you get the note I left on the fridge?"

"Yes Ma'am, and Sarah loved the breakfast you cooked this morning. It had her humming and dancing while she ate."

DeCarlos closed the door and headed for his 98' Honda Accord that his father gave him for passing his Driver's Test.

"Oh Yeah. So, she was doing the bank head bounce like she always does"

His mother said with a smile on her face. His mother loved compliments on her cooking.

"Yeah, you know it."

While talking to his mother he hears his phone beep twice.

"Hold on Ma I have someone on the other line" DeCarlos hurries up and clicks over to find out who it is.

"Hello"

Sarah asked, "Baby can you bring me some Rocky Road ice cream when you get back?"

"Ok I got you."

DeCarlos clicks back over to talk to his Ma.

"Ma you still there?"

"Yeah son, I'm still here. Is everything ok?"

"Everything's fine Ma, that was Sarah, she wanted me to get her some Rocky Road ice cream when I get back in the house."

"I see her cravings are flaring up early this morning" as his mom continues DeCarlos pulls off and heads toward school.

"Yeah ma, they sure are. But I'm not complaining, I like the experience."

"You like the experience now but wait until the baby comes. If you like the experience now you are going to *love* the experience, then."

"Ma, why is it that when you say it like that, I get a little worried."

"Because you should be"

"Ok Ma, I'm going to hang up now because you're starting to scare me a little."

DeCarlos could hear his mom starting to laugh which made him confused.

"DeCarlos, I didn't mean to scare you. I just wanted to make you aware of what's going to happen next"

"Ok Ma, got to go, love you."

"Love you too DeCarlos."

DeCarlos hung up the phone and began to think hard about what his mother said. DeCarlos pulled into the parking lot of Frederick Douglass High School, parked the car and sat there for a few seconds thinking of how hard it's going to be raising DeCarlos Jr.

"I need a job…" DeCarlos said to himself as he was getting out of the car. Just then the bell rang, signaling for class to start.

"Oh shit, I'm late."

CHAPTER 2

DeCarlos ran to his homeroom class. When he got there, he noticed the teacher was not in the room yet. So, he walked to the back of the class where his assigned seat was. He hung his book bag on the back of the chair and sat down. He took out a pencil and some paper and wrote on the top margin "Goals". On the first line under "Goals" he wrote "Job" and next to that he wrote "Own Place".

When DeCarlos looked up he noticed the girl sitting in front of him was turned around and staring at him.

"What's up Diane"

"Hey DeCarlos, what you writting?"

"I'm writing down goals that I need to accomplish so me and Sarah can get our own place."

"How's my best friend doing? I know she probably being a pain in the ass now. Having you run all over the place getting different types of food."

"You have no idea, Diane!"

"It's good to see you here. Most people I know around our age that have kids drop out of school and never see their kids."

"Well, that's not an option Diane. I have an ending in mind that I need to accomplish that only school will give me the steps for."

At that moment in comes Ms. Kirk the home room teacher.

"Ok students time to settle down" Ms. Kirk spoke in a loud voice as she put her briefcase on the desk in front of the class.

Ms. Kirk stood at the front of the class with her arms crossed, waiting for the students to finish their private conversations. While Ms. Kirk waited, DeCarlos sat at his desk staring out of the window wondering what job he should apply for. He almost came up with the perfect job but a white piece of folded up paper that was thrown on his desk broke his concentration.

DeCarlos looked up and noticed Diane turned around pointing at the

5

note. He grabbed it and opened it up underneath the desk so he wouldn't get caught by Ms. Kirk, it read:

You said you were writing down goals that you need to accomplish, what do you have down so far?

DeCarlos could hear Ms. Kirk calling the morning attendance as well as the students' responses to Ms. Kirk calling their names.

"Stephanie"

"Here."

"Cory,"

"Here."

"Portia,"

"Here."

"Toneah,"

"Here."

DeCarlos decided to wait for his name to be called before he wrote a response to Diane's note.

"Andrea,"

"Here."

"Jaqueline,"

"Here."

"DeCarlos,"

"Here." he replied.

After DeCarlos said here he took his pencil and wrote underneath Diane's message.

"All I have is this job for right now, maybe as the day goes by, I will have a few more."

DeCarlos folded up the letter and threw it under Diane's chair. Then to get her attention he tapped the back of her chair with his foot. This caused Diane to turn around and lock eyes with DeCarlos. DeCarlos pointed to the note underneath her chair. Diane turned her body sideways in the chair, reached down and acted like she was tying her shoe and at the same time she picked the note up off the floor. DeCarlos watched Diane as she read the note. I hope she don't pass the note back cause I'm not trying to get in trouble. DeCarlos thought as he went back to staring out the window.

He thought to himself, "If I get a job, then I can save up and buy me and Sarah a house. I could finally be on my own with my own family. I don't have to worry about the rules of the house, I can do what I want. If I get a job, then I won't have to ask for money anymore. I need some money; I need some money bad."

"DeCarlos, DeCarlos, DeCarlos" Ms. Kirk said repeatedly, trying to bring DeCarlos from out of his daze.

After hearing his name called repeatedly, he becomes aware of his surroundings.

"Yes ma'am"

"What's the answer?" Ms. Kirk asked.

It took DeCarlos a few seconds to even realize that Ms. Kirk asked a question in the first place. So, since he didn't have the answer, he did the next best thing. He guessed.

"Twenty-one"

At hearing the answer to Ms. Kirk's question every last student began to laugh.

"Quiet down students, quiet down" Ms. Kirk waited for the laughter to stop.

"DeCarlos from now on will you please pay attention in class?"

"Yes Ma'am, sorry about that"

DeCarlos leaned back in his chair and waited for the school bell to ring.

Riiiiiiiiiiinnngg.

DeCarlos grabbed his book bag and walked out the classroom where he met his friend Jeff. Jeff was a kid who was smart, his grade point average has been a 4.0 since he was a freshman. However, Jeff was so smart he was stupid.

"Jeff what's up slim?" DeCarlos said as he gave Jeff a handshake.

"Shit, coolin. What's up with you this morning?" Jeff said as they walked down the hallway towards DeCarlos' locker.

"Shit, coolin. Just wondering where I'm going to get this money so me and Sarah can move out of Dad and Mom's house. I know I need to get a job, but where am I going to work?"

"Work, job... Slim, you speaking Spanish to me. Check this out, at lunch time I need for you to do me a favor and I will give you two hundred dollars."

"Shit, I'm with it. I got a question though." DeCarlos replied.

"What's up?"

"Do we have to wait till lunchtime?"

This made Jeff laugh out loud.

"That's what I'm talking about Slim. I see you bout that money. Meet me by your car in ten minutes," said Jeff.

"Ok."

DeCarlos put his bookbag in his locker and walked out of the school to his car. He no longer thought about his grades or his parents. All he seen was dollar signs.

CHAPTER 3

"So, what's the deal Jeff?" DeCarlos asks.

"I need you to take me out to New Carlton Station right quick to meet up with some people."

"Ok I got you"

Jeff and DeCarlos hopped in the warm car and began to drive to New Carlton Station. DeCarlos cut the radio on and out came the smooth sounds of Alicia Keys. Jeff pulled out some O.G. Kush.

"Do you have any chocolates in here?"

DeCarlos pointed to the side of the seat that Jeff was sitting in, Jeff reached down in between the seat and the emergency break and pulled out a brown pack of chocolate flavored cigarillos. He took out one and smelled it.

"Damn I love the smell of chocolates"

Jeff began to break the blunt down the middle with his thumb nails.

"You have something I can put the guts in" Jeff asked looking around in the car.

DeCarlos pointed at the floor in the back. Jeff saw a Seven Eleven cup, got it and dumped the guts into it.

As DeCarlos listened to the words of Alicia Keys "Fallin", it made him think of Sarah and how much he loved her. He also began to think about what he could buy for his son.

Suddenly the smell of OG hit his nostrils. DeCarlos breathed in heavy. Oh, how I loved that smell he thought. Just then in his line of vision the nicely rolled weed filled Jay appeared.

"Here cuz" Jeff said.

DeCarlos grabbed the Jay, put it to his lips and inhaled deeply. He held the smoke in until he started coughing. Almost instantly his eyes turned red.

He gave the jay back to Jeff.

"That's what I'm talking about."

"Yeah, that's that ain't it."

All DeCarlos could do was shake his head up and down because he started coughing again.

"Did you see Diane today in school?" Jeff asked before puffing on the jay.

DeCarlos cut the music down just enough to be heard by the both of them.

"Yeah, I seen her. Why what's up?" DeCarlos asked.

"Slim, she was looking GOOD."

"I ain't even going to lie Slim, she was. Did you see her lips? Oh my God. I would love to suck that bottom lip"

"Shit me too!" Jeff exclaimed.

"Pass the jay."

Jeff passed the jay to DeCarlos. And cracked the window to let the smoke out.

"How's Sarah doing?" He asked.

"She's good, she's having these crazy cravings though. Just this morning she asked me to get her some Rocky Road ice cream when I get in the house and that was six thirty this morning. Who thinks about ice cream at six thirty in the morning?"

"I guess Sarah does."

"Can I be honest with you Jeff?"

"DeCarlos, I have known you my whole life there's no reason you can't be honest."

"Slim, all I been thinking about is getting out of my parents' house. Getting somewhere that me and Sarah can enjoy without my parents being in my business all the time."

"I understand where you are coming from but hold on, I need to call someone."

"Ok"

Jeff pulled out his phone from his jean pants pocket and began dialing numbers. While Jeff was on the phone talking, DeCarlos fell into a state of depression. He didn't know what to do to get him and Sarah away from the house.

Jeff got off the phone, "they said meet them at the top of New Carlton Station. Pull up by the gate."

"ok"

"But nah what I was saying was I know you want to get out the house and take care of Sarah and DeCarlos Jr. on your own but trust me when I say it's going to take some time. It's not going to happen overnight. Not unless you rob a bank or something. But if you stick with me, I can help you accomplish your goal."

Jeff's phone rang and he put it on speaker phone.

"Hello"

"You there" The voice said

"Yeah, I'm here, where are you?"

Jeff looked out the window towards the station trying to pick his mans out of the crowd.

"I'm leaning against the steps; do you see me?"

Jeff looked towards the steps and spotted his man before speaking into the phone.

"On my way", "let's go DeCarlos"

DeCarlos and Jeff got out of the car and walked towards the steps where they met a young male. Jeff extended his hand.

"What's up John?"

"What's up Jeff?" John looks at DeCarlos with a puzzled look and nods towards DeCarlos.

"Who dis bruh?"

"Oh, this is my mans DeCarlos, he cool."

"ok. What's up Bruh?"

John reaches out to give DeCarlos a handshake.

"What's up Slim?" DeCarlos said as he gave John a firm grip handshake.

John turns to Jeff.

"Hey Jeff, you got that?"

"Yeah, I got it, you got the money?"

"Don't I always?"

"Jeff, you got some tree on you?"

"Yeah."

"I'll match you one."

"I'm with it," Jeff said.

DeCarlos, Jeff and John all head back to DeCarlos' car. On the way back to the car, John keeps looking at DeCarlos as if he looks familiar.

"Hey DeCarlos, what school you go to?"

"Douglass, you?"

"I go to Wise. You know someone named Sarah? She white with blonde hair and has emerald, green eyes." DeCarlos pauses for a moment acting as if he was in deep thought before opening up the driver's side door.

"Nah, I don't know no Tarah, she sound bad though. Hey John, sit up front with me. I wanna hear about this Tarah chick. She got my nose open just hearing about what she look like" Jeff said.

DeCarlos gets in the car and unlocks the doors. As Jeff and John get in the car DeCarlos reaches under his seat and grabs a pack of chocolates. He hands the pack to Jeff who sits behind John.

"Twist one of those, then hand the other one to John."

"Her name was Sarah not Tarah" John said in a defensive tone.

"My bad Slim. I didn't mean no harm"

"It's cool. Players make mistakes too, but like I was saying Sarah is sexy as shit. She has a fat oh ass too. I mean it's huge."

At hearing this DeCarlos starts to feel good, he even begins to smile a little. He liked the fact that his girl was still wanted by other people. DeCarlos begins to wonder how John knows her. He decides not to ask because he doesn't want to let John know she is his girl and she's pregnant with his son. So, he just lets him talk. They pass the jays around and talk for several minutes and then John's phone rings.

"Hello... aight I'll be there in five minutes."

"Hey Jeff, I need to go take care of some business, we going to do this or what?"

"Let me count the money first."

John reaches in his pocket and hands Jeff a wad of money. DeCarlos looks on wide eyed as Jeff counts the money in front of him. After Jeff finishes counting the money, he looks at John in the front seat.

"Look under the seat. Brown paper bag!"

John reaches under the seat and pulls out the brown paper bag. Looks inside and pulls out some of its contents. He opens a sandwich bag and sticks his pink nail inside, then he puts his nails in his mouth. After a few seconds he begins to shake his head up and down satisfied with what he's got.

Jeff looks at John as he shakes his head and knows he likes what he got but decides to ask anyway to see what he is going to say.

"You like?"

John turns in the seat to face Jeff with a smile on his face.

"*Meeeee liiiiike*"

"You're a straight up bamma but aight cool, I've got business to handle as well."

Jeff and John shake hands and then John and DeCarlos shake hands.

"Imma get at yall later."

When John gets out of the car so does Jeff with a lit jay in his mouth. Jeff opens the front door and gets in.

"Slim why you ain't cut the heat on, it's freezing in here"

Jeff pulls up the hood on his coat. DeCarlos hears Jeff loud and clear. He grabs the jay from Jeff and takes a couple of puffs then he cuts the heat on and rolls up the windows.

"You hungry DeCarlos?"

"Hell yeah, what you got in mind?"

"Let's go up the street and grab some Popeyes"

"Shit I'm with it"

DeCarlos drives to the Popeyes up the street by the liquor store. He rolls down the window and tosses the roach before entering the drive thru which is a couple of cars long. While they wait for the line to die down some, DeCarlos decides to do a little information digging. So, he thinks for a few seconds about where to begin. He glances over at Jeff who is counting his money.

"Jeff, how you know John? "Jeff looks up with a puzzling look on his face.

"Why, what's up DeCarlos? What's going on in that little mind of yours?"

"Naw I'm just wondering how you know him, maybe that can tell me how he knows Sarah."

"So that's the real reason. You want to know how he knows Sarah"

"Yeah, I do."

"Ok I'm going to give you both answers, but you need to remember you asked for it. First, order the food."

DeCarlos eases up to the window where a light skinned female with a black ponytail that comes down to the middle of her back takes their order.

"Welcome to Popeyes, how can I help you?"

DeCarlos looks at the menu for a few seconds and then back at the cashier. He notices her name tag reads Erika.

"Can I get a ten-piece bucket of chicken? All breast and thighs please, with a side of mashed potatoes"

Erika repeatedly taps the computer screen to punch in DeCarlos' order.

"Hey Erika" DeCarlos said and waits until Erika is looking him dead in his eyes.

"Can you make sure that all I get is breasts and thighs?"

Erika takes one look at DeCarlos and rolls her eyes.

"Yeah, I will make sure that's *all* you get." She said in a smart voice before putting her hands on her hips.

DeCarlos just smiled knowing that his advances were just shot down.

"Hey Jeff, what you want?"

"Let me get the same thing my homie just ordered," Jeff said while leaning over DeCarlos so he can see Erika.

While Erika is putting the order into the computer, Jeff hands DeCarlos a wad of cash.

"Show her the money and watch her hop on your line."

"I got you cuz" DeCarlos

Erika turns to face DeCarlos and Jeff.

"That will be fifteen, seventy-five" Erika said to DeCarlos.

DeCarlos holds the money so that Erika can see him counting it out without looking like he is trying to show off.

At seeing the wad of money Erika begins to cough slightly amazed at what is going on in front of her. DeCarlos can see she is staring at the wad of cash, so he counts it slowly out for her then hands her a twenty-dollar bill.

Erika takes the money and then tries to give DeCarlos his change.

"Naw that's okay beautiful, you keep it. I don't like having anything under a twenty in my pockets"

"Oh ok, thank you Daddy."

Erika leans forward a little and pokes out her chest.

"Would you like anything else?"

DeCarlos takes out his cell phone and hangs it out the window in front of her.

"Your number would be fine for now."

Erika begins to smile.

"Ok."

Erika takes the phone and puts in her contact information and hands the phone back along with their order.

"Talk to you later, Daddy."

DeCarlos didn't respond, he just pulled off laughing at her. And headed to the gas station down the street. Jeff turned and looked at DeCarlos.

"I told you she was going to bite. All they respect is money, money makes the world go round. Speaking of money, Nigga give me mines back"

DeCarlos handed Jeff the wad of cash as Jeff peeled off two hundred dollars.

"Here is the money I promised."

DeCarlos pulled into the gas station and parked in front of the entrance.

"Okay enough play time. Are you going to tell me how you know John and how he knows Sarah or naw?"

DeCarlos said getting back on the topic. They both got out and headed inside.

"I was wondering when you were going to ask about that. But yeah, I know John from Douglass, he did his freshman year there before he got transferred to Wise."

"Why don't I know him then?"

"He hung out with the chess team."

"Oh, that's why."

DeCarlos headed to the back freezer and grabbed a pint of Rocky Road ice cream then he went and got four 99 cent soda's and headed to the cash register. After paying for the merchandise, they headed back to the car and got in.

"You still haven't told me how John knows Sarah" DeCarlos asks with a mouthful of chicken.

"John use to fuck Sarah. You couldn't tell, look at how he got defensive when you fucked up her name"

DeCarlos went silent. And immediately made up his mind that he didn't like John. Even though he didn't know anything about him. Jeff seen DeCarlos moving around like he was uncomfortable in the driver's seat. He also noticed that DeCarlos went from happy to upset as soon as he mentioned John use to fuck Sarah.

"Slim, get out your feelings. It happened before you and Sarah got together."

"Man, I ain't trippin off that shit Slim. Like you said, 'It happened before me, and Sarah even got together"

Jeff knew DeCarlos was lying but he chose not to feed into his lie. So, he decided to change the topic.

"Aight cool, it's only twelve o'clock, so what's the next move?"

"Shiiiit, I only brought you out here so you can handle business and plus I needed the money."

DeCarlos started up the car and headed back to Upper Marlboro. On the way there the car was absolutely quiet which gave DeCarlos time to think about his next move. He glanced over at Jeff and noticed him playing on his cell phone.

"Hey Jeff, what you playing over there?"

"Candy Crush."

"Candy Crush, of all the things you could have downloaded on Google Play, you choose Candy Crush"

The thought of Jeff actually playing Candy Crush made DeCarlos giggle a little bit.

"Jeff twist up a jay for me right quick."

"Aight, I got you."

Jeff put his phone down, got some weed out the glove compartment, grabbed the chocolates off the floor and began to roll the weed.

"Jeff my bad about earlier. And good looking with this money. Next time you need to come out here, let me know, I'm wit it. As long as the money stays the same or gets better."

"You want better. I just put two hundred dollars in your pocket and you talkin about better"

"No offense Slim, but more money ain't never hurt nobody"

"Ok if that's the way you feel, how would you like to make a stack tonight?"

DeCarlos looked over at Jeff while eating a piece of chicken and with crumbs on his face said:

"Like I told you, I'm wit it."

DeCarlos pulled up to the house and parked in the driveway.

"I have to meet up with someone around five, I want you to go with me"

DeCarlos and Jeff get out the car, grabbed the sodas, chicken and ice cream from out the back seat and walked up to the front door.

"Be careful Jeff, the sidewalk is slippery as shit, I didn't put enough salt down last night."

DeCarlos took out his keys and opened the front door.

"Make sure you toss that roach before you come inside" DeCarlos said as he noticed the lit Jay in Jeff's hand. Jeff looked down at his hand before stepping into the house.

"Damn my bad Slim. I ain't even know I had it in my hand"

DeCarlos looked at Jeff and started to shake his head slowly.

"Nigga, you really, need to stop smoking"

Jeff flicked the roach into the yard went inside and went straight for the fridge. After DeCarlos locked the front door, he walked to the kitchen and noticed Jeff neck deep in the fridge.

"Move nigga, I got to put the soda in there"

Jeff moved out of the way so DeCarlos could put the soda in.

"Damn Slim, I'm high as shit. My mouth dry as shit too."

You know where they cups at nigga, get you some water."

"I'm a guest in your house, you ain't going to get it for me?"

DeCarlos looked at Jeff with that nigga please look. Grabbed the Ice cream and a spoon out of the drawer and began to walk off to find Sarah. Jeff yelled as DeCarlos disappeared around the corner.

"I know your mother taught you better manners than that"

At the top of the steps DeCarlos shouted back.

"Yeah, she did but she ain't here is she"

Then DeCarlos focused on finding Sarah.

"Sarah, Sarah, where you at baby?"

"I'm in the bathroom" Sarah yelled

DeCarlos walked to the bathroom and turned the knob to find out it was locked, so he knocked against the door.

"You ok baby?"

"Yeah, I'm fine, just taking a piss right quick" Sarah said from the other side.

"I got something for you"

DeCarlos heard the toilet flush and then the sink run and a few seconds later he saw the doorknob turn. DeCarlos put the spoon and the Ice cream behind his back.

Sarah came out the bathroom with a smile on her face and her hands out.

"What you got for me?"

"Oh, you're going to love this. I'm going to give you a clue. It's silver and it's medium length. You can use it every day, well almost every day."

At hearing this Sarah's face went from happy to immediate confusion. DeCarlos saw the confused look on Sarah's face and immediately started laughing.

"Boy what's so funny?"

"You," he replied, looking Sarah directly in her eyes.

Sarah put her hands on her hip and caught an attitude.

"Why am I funny?"

"You should have seen your face when I said silver and medium length.

You're face when from happy to confused as shit so fast"

DeCarlos kept laughing while he was talking which made Sarah even more mad.

"Oh, quit the games. What you got for me?"

DeCarlos held up the spoon so Sarah could see it.

"Here is what I got for you"

When Sarah laid eyes on the spoon her face immediately turned red with rage. DeCarlos could see her getting madder and madder.

"Boy what the fuck I need with a goddamn spoon?"

Hearing Sarah start cussing and seeing her face turn red made DeCarlos fall on the floor with laughter.

Sarah looked at DeCarlos like he was crazy then noticed the pint of ice cream next to him. It took her a couple of seconds for her to realize that he just finished playing a little joke on her. When it finally hit her, she began to smile. She walked over to DeCarlos and softly kissed him on his lips.

"I should beat your ass for playing with me like that, now give me my ice cream"

DeCarlos got up off the floor with tears in his eyes and walked to the bathroom and rinsed off the spoon. Grabbed the ice cream off the floor and gave Sarah a kiss on the forehead.

"My bad baby. It's just funny as shit watching you get mad for no reason. You look like a cherry with a ponytail."

DeCarlos handed Sarah the ice cream and the spoon.

"Thank you, baby, and fuck you." Sarah said as she walked to the bedroom.

DeCarlos looked at her as she walked off.

"Anytime baby, anytime"

This made Sarah smile knowing that even though she was getting big her man still wanted her. After they made it to the bedroom Sarah crawled into bed and DeCarlos sat next to her.

"Oh, by the way, Jeff is here. He is in the kitchen probably drowning himself in orange soda and look for something else to eat"

"Why, y'all just finish smoking?" Sarah asked as she began to eat the ice cream.

"Yeah, we hit a couple jays on the way to the store and on the way back."

"I could tell, I smell it on your clothes."

DeCarlos notices that the T.V. was on a commercial.

"What you watching?"

"Jerry Springer"

"Re-run"

"Yeah"

DeCarlos looked at his watch, it was going on two o'clock.

"Yo, I need to get back to school before they decide to call Ma and tell her I didn't show up today."

DeCarlos leaned over and kissed Sarah on the forehead.

"See you later baby"

"Aight see you when you get back" Sarah said with a mouthful of ice cream.

DeCarlos began to leave out of the room but before he made it to the door, he remembered something.

"Oh, baby me and Jeff are going to be going out around four-thirty, five o'clock, we have something we need to do."

Sarah looked at DeCarlos with a puzzled look on her face. She wanted to ask what they had planned but had a feeling she shouldn't get into his business.

"Ok yall, stay safe out there tonight."

Sarah watched DeCarlos walk out of the room and could hear his footsteps going down the stairs.

Sarah closed her eyes for a quick sec to say a prayer.

"Lord please don't let that boy get into trouble and end up leaving me to take care of this baby by myself. This baby shouldn't have to grow up without a father so please keep him safe lord, please"

Meanwhile downstairs in the kitchen DeCarlos sits on the counter and begins to talk to Jeff.

"Don't drink up all my orange soda fool."

"Nigga stop tripping"

Jeff put the orange soda back into the fridge while DeCarlos hopped down from off the counter.

"Come on Jeff we need to get back to school before they start tripping"

Jeff turned to look at DeCarlos

"The school is the last person you need to worry about. You need to worry about Ma. She the one that's going to knock you into next year if she finds out you ain't in school. You remember the time when she came to the school and embarrassed you in front of everybody. She jacked you up and told you to pay attention, remember that?"

Hearing this made DeCarlos laugh because he knew Jeff was telling the truth. DeCarlos and Jeff headed to the car.

"Hey DeCarlos after school, kick it with me, I have to run by my house before we go out tonight."

"Aight, I got you."

DeCarlos and Jeff hop in the car and head to school.

CHAPTER 4

DeCarlos pulled up to school and parked in his normal parking space. DeCarlos and Jeff got out of the car and rushed to the back door of the school. They passed the football team as they were practicing and ran into the school. As they were running through the halls to get to class DeCarlos turns and looks at Jeff.

"Meet me at the car after school Slim."

"Aight DeCarlos, I got you."

They separated ways, Jeff heads towards his class as DeCarlos heads to his. On his way into class DeCarlos saw Diane standing in front of his last period class talking to the school principal. He slows down from a run to a walk. As DeCarlos gets within earshot the principal begins to talk to him.

"Hey DeCarlos, nice for you to finally drop in."

"Hey Ms. Proctor, what you talking about? I was in the bathroom."

"That's what I told her, but she didn't believe me" Diane said.

DeCarlos looks at the principle and back to Diane.

"Why y'all talking about me anyway?"

"Your mother called me and asked for me to check up on you. She had a feeling you were up to something." Ms. Proctor said with her arms crossed.

"Well, you can call her back and tell her I'm fine, just a little constipated that's all."

Ms. Procter took a look at DeCarlos and rolled her eyes. She could tell he was lying but decided that it was not worth the paperwork, after all school was almost over for the day anyway.

"Ok DeCarlos if you say so. You may need to take something for that constipation. It's causing you to miss class."

"You may be right Ms. Procter, now that I think about it. If I take something I can get more work done and in turn I can get better grades and possibly get into Howard University."

"You want to go to Howard?" I didn't know that DeCarlos." Diane said with a look of surprise on her face, Ms. Procter had the same exact look but voiced her surprise.

"DeCarlos, that's a real surprise. I never figured you as a Howard graduate. Maybe a PG Community College or maybe even a UDC person."

Now DeCarlos was the one with a perplexed look on his face. He looked at Diane first

Then back to Mrs. Proctor.

"I don't know if I should take that as a compliment or an insult so I'm going to leave it alone and ask, why is that?"

"Because I see you work hard in class, however I don't see you doing anything extra outside of class to give you the discipline you need to get a full scholarship to Howard. And before you say anything else, remember me and your mother are like this."

Mrs. Proctor holds up her hand and crosses her fingers. To let DeCarlos know how close. And without saying anything else Mr. Proctor walked off.

Just then the school bell rang, signaling the school day was over.

[Ring, Ring, Ring}

"DeCarlos, what made you want to go to Howard?" Diane asked while clutching her books close to her chest as kids began to file out of the classrooms all at once.

"Well to be honest Diane, none of my parents went to college. And I think it will be my chance to really do something with myself. A chance to get out the neighborhood you know?"

"Yeah, I understand DeCarlos. If I go to college, I will be the first out of my family as well. The only difference between me and you as far as college goes is, I never thought about Howard. I always thought about community college, you know, Prince George's Community College maybe. It's only up the street and around the corner."

"Diane, I have two questions for you. I noticed you said if you go to college. Why did you say if? I have known you since middle school and you have always got good grades. You may have struggled in some classes but good grades all in all. You work hard and you don't allow your friends to steer you in anyway, you don't want to go. And yeah, I remember your parents' divorce and the death of your younger brother."

When Diane heard that she lowered her head and began to stare at her feet. She loved her brother and wishes he was still around.

DeCarlos picked up on her emotional change.

"Diane, look at me please."

Diane lifted her head up slowly and looked DeCarlos in the eye.

"Diane college is not an option for you, it's a must. You must change history. You must leave the hood. You must do something to get your parents out of this hell hole we call home. And you must."

DeCarlos paused to make sure he had Diane's full attention. When he felt like he did, he began to smile, and continued.

"And you must give your brother a reason to smile. Cause he is watching your success. You can count on it."

Hearing DeCarlos speak of her brother made Diane smile. She felt better about going to college and talking to DeCarlos.

"I see that smile that got all the bamma niggas going crazy is back. You must be feeling a lot better."

DeCarlos put his arm around Diane and Diane playfully hit DeCarlos in the chest.

"Boy shut up, don't hate. And yes, I do feel better, thank you for caring."

It was DeCarlos' turn to laugh. With his arm still around Diane he said.

"Girl I ain't say I cared. I was just being the gentleman that my pops raised me to be, that's all."

Diane rolled her eyes.

"Yeah whatever." she said with a smile

Diane and DeCarlos paused for a few seconds. DeCarlos removed his arm and looked around. And he saw no one in the hallway, then he turned to look at Diane.

"Diane, do you got a ride home?"

"If you plan on taking me home, I do."

"Yeah, I can do that."

They begin to walk to DeCarlos' car. Just then DeCarlos' phone rang, and he picked up.

"Hello?"

"Yeah, I'm on the way to the car now."

"Aight, I'll wait for you."

On the way to the car, DeCarlos decided to ask the second question.

"Diane, I said I had two questions. The other question is why don't you shoot for the stars as far as college is concerned?"

Diane and DeCarlos walked across the parking lot in silence. Diane didn't really know what DeCarlos was talking about, so she stayed quiet. By the time DeCarlos and Diane got to the car, DeCarlos picked up on the reason Diane was quiet. DeCarlos began to unlock the door to the car.

"Diane, if you have any questions, you know you can always ask them. Don't be afraid to talk ok." Diane began to get into the front seat.

"Naw Diane, don't even think about it, get in the back seat."

"What! Why?"

"Cause I said so. Don't question your ride home. I'll leave you right where you stand, now get in the back seat."

Diane got in the back seat as told. DeCarlos hopped in and cut the heat on and decided to explain his question.

"What I meant by shooting for the stars is why don't you set a goal of going to a big college, that way if you don't make it, at least you will still have the GPA and credits to get into a decent college."

While Diane was thinking, DeCarlos decided to roll a jay and spark it. DeCarlos turns around to Diane and waits for an answer.

"Diane, you smoke?"

DeCarlos held up the jay and waited to see how quick she was going to answer the question.

"Yeah, I smoke" Diane reached for the jay and DeCarlos pulled it away.

"Not before you answer the question!"

"Ok fine"

Just then Jeff got into the car.

"Oh, yall got it smelling good as fuck in here. What's up Diane?"

"What's up Jeff?"

DeCarlos passed the jay to Jeff.

"Oh, you just going to say fuck me" Diane said catching an attitude about not getting the jay passed to her.

Jeff began to pass the jay to Diane.

"Oh, naw Jeff, don't give her that jay. I told her she can't smoke until she tells me why she won't set a goal of going to some place like Yale or Harvard that way if she don't make it, at least she will get accepted to a college that still holds some weight in this world."

After hearing this Jeff shook his head up and down in agreement while inhaling the jay twice and then blowing the smoke in Diane's face. Diane wanted to smoke so bad, so she spoke her mind.

"First of all, yall not about to play with me like I'm some type of bird brain bitch. So, let's make that clear right now."

She paused to make sure that Jeff and DeCarlos understood what she was saying and then she continued.

"DeCarlos, I understand where you are coming from. If I shoot for the stars at least I will land on the clouds. It's just that I don't think I have what it takes to get to the stars.

DeCarlos started the car up and began to drive Diane home. Jeff handed the jay to Diane.

"Enjoy, you earned it."

"Fuck you Jeff" Diane said before she leaned back and puffed on the jay.

"Diane, I never knew you didn't have confidence in yourself." DeCarlos said.

"Well, I don't"

DeCarlos looked in the rearview mirror at Diane and they locked eyes.

"Just give it sometime and you will have all the confidence you will need. Before you know it, you will be grown, looking hella good and enjoying life. Once you set and reach your goal everything else falls into place. One of these days I'm going to get with you, and we are going to have a serious talk, just me and you, ok?"

"Ok"

"But for now, let's just enjoy the high"

DeCarlos, Diane and Jeff all shook their heads in agreement and set back and enjoyed the ride. Twenty minutes later they were pulling in front of Diane's house. Diane got out of the back seat and leaned into the window.

"See you tomorrow and tell Sarah I said hi"

"I got you," DeCarlos said.

Jeff watched as Diane walked to the front door of her house. After she got inside Jeff turned to DeCarlos.

"Damn she is so sexy. I would love to hit that."

DeCarlos and Jeff started to laugh as DeCarlos pulled off and headed to Jeff's house.

CHAPTER 5

After three days and a few shared memories DeCarlos finally pulled into Jeff's driveway and parked the car and went inside and headed straight for the kitchen. He walked right past Jeff's mother at the stove making dinner, opened the fridge and went straight for the orange soda. And without any hesitation he opened the bottle and began to drink.

"I see someone's thirsty from all the weed," Jeff's mother said as she watched DeCarlos drinking from the bottle of the fridge.

Hearing the voice made DeCarlos jump and caused him to spill soda on his shirt.

"Damn it"

DeCarlos said as he began to wipe off his shirt while turning toward the voice. Once he realized who it was, he felt a little guilty.

"Oh hey Ms. Stephanie. I didn't know you were standing there. Sorry about not using the cups, I'm just really thirsty."

"I can see that. I also see your eyes are as red as the bottom of my heels. And you smell like a marijuana factory. However, now that you have apologized why don't you put the soda down and grab a cup. You know where they are."

"Yes ma'am"

DeCarlos put the soda down and grabbed the cup from out of the cabinet. Ms. Stephanie began to giggle a little bit, because she began to think about when she used to do the same thing. The thought only lasted a quick second then she turned back to the stove to finish cooking dinner. Jeff walked in the kitchen and snuck up behind his mother, wrapped his arms around her and gave her a kiss on the cheek.

"Hey Ma"

"Hey son. You smell like a weed factory too. Damn, yall was getting it in"

Ms. Stephanie turned around to take a look at her son, his eyes most of all. The eyes always tell the story. Jeff picked up on his mother's eyes immediately. He knew he was under observation, so he dug in his pocket and took out five hundred dollars and put it on the kitchen table next to his mom and changed the subject.

"Somebody's in a good mood for once, you're making my favorite, spaghetti."

Then he looks a little closer at her and notices she was not in her work clothes.

"And you're not in your regular clothes, where you been at lady?"

"I see, even though you are high you are still very observant"

Ms. Stephanie began to smile. He reminded her of his father, he always paid attention to detail.

"To answer your question, I went out to get drinks with a friend. That's all you need to know, nosy."

DeCarlos decided to chip in on the conversation, deciding to try and get himself out of hot water.

"Did you have a good time"

"Yes DeCarlos, I actually did thanks for asking. But you don't get off that easy. Next time you come in my house and don't use a cup, Imma stick my foot up your hind parts, you understand?"

DeCarlos looks down at his feet.

"Yes Ma'am."

There was a short pause then Jeff and DeCarlos took that as the queue to get out of the kitchen and head to Jeff's room. DeCarlos took off his coat and hung it up in the closet.

"DeCarlos, lock the door for me."

"Aight."

DeCarlos locked the door and began to wonder what the hell was going on. He sat down at the edge of the bed and watched Jeff move around in his room.

"DeCarlos, look in the top drawer and take the weed out and then look in the second drawer and take out the blunts. We about to smoke."

DeCarlos got up and did just that. He began to twist up a Jay while Jeff checked his watch. It was four o'clock.

"Ok we got about thirty minutes to chill before we have to head out. Go ahead and spark that up so I can run down what is about to take place."

Jeff said as he sat down in the chair next to the bed facing DeCarlos.

After about ten minutes of silence with nothing but the smell of intoxicating weed to fill the space Jeff decided to speak.

"Ok this is what's going to happen. We are going to take a couple of guns to a good friend of mine out of VA and in turn we are going to get a couple guns that are going to be fresh out of the box."

He stopped.

"DeCarlos, have you ever seen a real gun before?"

DeCarlos looked as if Jeff was nuts.

"Nigga. I might be green to this shit but I ain't forest green nigga"

"Ok have you ever used a gun before?"

"To shoot someone, no. But I have used one just for target practice." DeCarlos said, with less confidence that he had in his voice than before.

"That's good enough. Look under the bed and grab the duffle bag for me. Then put them gloves on that are under my pillow."

DeCarlos grabbed the bag and tossed it to Jeff's feet. Jeff got up and grabbed a pair of rubber gloves from out of his dresser and sat back down. He then unzipped the bag and emptied the contents out onto the floor. DeCarlos tried to act like he saw stuff like this all the time, but he couldn't keep his composure. His eyes widened as Jeff poured out fifteen to twenty handguns.

DeCarlos reached out and grabbed one. It was chrome with a blueish gray pearl handle and could fit in the palm of his hand. He held it up to the light and moved it back and forth and fell in love with how the light bounced off of it. He loved the size of the gun too. It was the perfect size to fit in his front pocket without really showing. The perfect concealed weapon he thought.

Jeff noticed that DeCarlos was in a trance.

"Chill slim. I promise you, one day I will get you one just like it. But it can't be that one. The guns you see in front of you are dirty. That means they have already been used to commit a crime and if you get caught with it, they can blame the crime or crimes on you no matter what it is.

It could be a murder or just a simple drive bye, you get caught with it you wear it. You hear me DeCarlos?"

"I ain't stupid nigga. You have known me for several years and you say that

I feel offended"

DeCarlos said, putting his hand up to his chest as if he was hurt.

"Don't be, just had to say it. It made me feel better. We cool?"

Jeff extended his hand to DeCarlos to shake.

"Cool" DeCarlos reached out and gave him a handshake.

"Jeff, why we droppin' off guns to pick up guns?"

"Ok. This is how it works. I buy guns from a dealer then I sell those guns to some of my associates. After my associates use the guns in any way, they see fit. I buy them back for a fraction of the price I sold them for. You following me?"

DeCarlos sits on the bed wide-eyed listening to every word.

"Yeah, I follow"

"Ok. Then when I get enough guns, I go back to the dealer and pay him a fraction of what I bought them back for so he can change the grips and do a little more magic in the guns so when someone gets pulled over with them, they are not linked to a crime.

I also get the serial numbers shaved off, so they won't be traceable. Then I turn around and sell them to other people or on some occasions I would sell the guns right back.

So, say if I paid three hundred for a gun, I would sell it for six. And after it was used, I would go buy it back for around one-hundred and fifty then I would get it fixed for about fifty bucks so all in all I would only pay about five hundred for it the first go around then after that it pays for itself. One hundred percent profit. Can't go wrong with free money"

DeCarlos looked at Jeff amazed but also confused.

"Jeff, you think like that why don't you get a job and stack money or start a legal business"

Jeff stood up.

"Cause a job won't help my moms like she need it. And one day I'm going to buy my mom's a big ass house. Just wait and see"

"Nigga why you ain't got a car yet, all that money you getting" DeCarlos said half in humor and half serious.

"Cause, I'm saving up to buy my moms a house didn't you hear anything I just said"

"Yeah, I did, but—"

"But what?" Jeff said in an angry voice.

"Never mind let's get this money"

"Now you talking my language cuz," Jeff looked at his watch and it was four thirty. Jeff began to put the guns in the bag.

"Hey DeCarlos, keep them gloves in your pocket. I need for you to take me down to Forest Heights Mall so I can get a car right quick. Don't want to use yours ya dig?" DeCarlos gets up and stretches.

"Yeah, I dig, so let's go then, we got thirty minutes till we got to meet up with your peoples."

They run to DeCarlos' car to kill time. In five minutes they arrive at the parking lot.

"Ok check this out Imma need you to park in the middle of the parking lot after you drop me off at this corner. Imma need for you to watch my back if you see anyone coming towards me lay on that horn like your life depends on it. When you see me pulling out the parking space, I want you to follow me back to the crib"

"Aight, I got you"

DeCarlos dropped Jeff off at the corner of the Burlington Coat Factory right by the Key Store and went to go park in the middle of the parking lot.

He watched as Jeff crept threw the cars like a skilled pro, making sure no one was following him or paying him any attention. Once Jeff reached the car, he was looking for he raised his elbow and smashed out the driver's side window. Then he slowly slid the door open and crept inside, careful not to attract too much attention. Once he was inside, he took out a flat head screwdriver and began to do his thing. And when he was done, he pulled out the parking lot as DeCarlos followed. They went down Pennsylvania Ave doing 80 miles per hour, weaving in and out of traffic.

When they got to Jeff's house DeCarlos parked his car and Jeff ran in the house to get his duffle bag. While Jeff was in the house DeCarlos put on his gloves and hopped into the driver's side of the stolen car. He pulled out a chocolate and some weed and rolled a jay. While he waited, he lit the jay and looked at his watch. It was five o'clock on the nose.

DeCarlos beeped the horn twice and Jeff came running out with the duffle bag on his shoulder and got into the car. Got his phone and called his contact. After getting the schedule back on track he hung up the phone and grabbed the jay from DeCarlos.

"King St. Alexandria VA"

DeCarlos took out his cell phone and punched in the coordinates on MapQuest. After the directions came up, he pulled off.

"Let me see your phone right quick," DeCarlos asked Jeff.

Jeff handed him the phone. DeCarlos dialed Sarah's cell phone number and she picked up on the first ring.

"Hello"

"Hey baby it's me I have you on speaker. You, ok?" DeCarlos said while driving.

"Yeah, I'm good baby, how you holding up?"

"I'm good, chasing this money"

"You out with Jeff?"

"Yeah. I'm driving right now, just wanted to hear your voice and make sure everything was good"

"Aww that's so sweet. Love you too baby. Jeff keep my baby father out of trouble, you hear me!"

Jeff passed the jay to DeCarlos

"I ain't tryna hear that shit you kickin right now I'm tryna get something to eat" Jeff said to Sarah.

"Please don't mention food right now"

"Ok I won't, but we going to Popeyes to get a big ass bucket of extra crispy spicy chicken and some soda."

"Damn it DeCarlos call me when you're not around the asshole"

"Ok Baby, talk to you later"

DeCarlos hung up the phone and started laughing.

"Jeff, you wrong as shit for that one"

"It had to be done. We have to keep our mind on business ok. Until we get back in one piece. Speaking of peace, I have a Glock nine under your seat just in case we need it ok?"

"Aight"

DeCarlos and Jeff rode in complete silence until they got to King Street Metro Station.

"There he goes over there in the brown van" Jeff said as he pointed in the direction of the van.

DeCarlos pulls up to the side of the van.

"DeCarlos grab the gun and keep it in your jacket pocket with your finger on the trigger, ok?"

DeCarlos reached down and got the gun and put it in his pocket.

"I got you cuz"

The driver's side window rolled down on the van and a young female began to talk.

"What's up Jeff, hope all is well. How about you and your friend hop in the back"

DeCarlos and Jeff got out of the car and hopped in the back of the van without any questions.

The girl that was driving came to the back and sat across from DeCarlos. DeCarlos' mouth hung open in awe at how pretty she was. She was a Spanish and Black woman with long curly hair like he likes it. Small waist, nice curves, real pink lips and a cocoa butter skin complexion. She wore all blue.

"Who is your friend Jeff?" the girl said.

Without waiting on an introduction from Jeff.

"Hey, I'm DeCarlos what's your name?"

"They call me Angel, nice to meet you handsome" Angel said with a wink.

DeCarlos picked up on the slight flirting she was doing.

"Believe me the pleasure is all mine," DeCarlos said.

"Ok Jeff let's get down to business shall we" Angel said in a serious tone.

"Let's," Jeff replied.

Jeff opened the duffle bag and showed Angel what he needed. They agreed on a price and then Angel gave Jeff another duffle bag. This one was bigger and longer. Jeff looked inside and gave Angel a head nod.

"See you next time, later Angel"

'Ok and make sure you bring handsome here with you"

"It's a deal" Jeff said.

"Bye DeCarlos" Angel said with a slight smile on her face.

"Bye Beautiful"

DeCarlos and Jeff hopped out the van and into the car and headed back across state lines. DeCarlos looked at Jeff.

"Now that was pretty easy wasn't it" DeCarlos said to Jeff.

"DeCarlos it is not over till we are home. Were the tree though?"

Jeff got an urge to get high that had to be taken care of.

DeCarlos pulled out some weed and another chocolate so Jeff can twist it up. DeCarlos and Jeff smoked the whole way back to Jeff's crib. They pulled up to the driveway and Jeff got out and ran the duffle bag inside and was back out in sixty seconds.

"Ok DeCarlos time to dump the car," Jeff said getting into the driver's seat.

"Aight."

Jeff drove the car for about ten minutes and then pulled over to the side of the road on a residential street. He grabbed some pieces of paper and a lighter. He scattered sheets of paper all over the inside of the car and then grabbed a gas can from out of the trunk and completely drenched the inside of the car as well as the outside. Took the lighter and set the car on fire then got into DeCarlos' car and they drove off back to Jeff's crib.

They went into Jeff's room and sat back for a while. Now they could breathe a lot better. Jeff opened the duffle bag and there was two AK-47s, an Uzi, and a Tech Nine. Jeff looked up and saw DeCarlos eyeballing his guns. So, he grabbed two thousand dollars out his dresser and threw it to DeCarlos.

"Our business is done for today, time for you to go home DeCarlos"

DeCarlos caught it and put it in his pockets, got up and left.

"Aight talk to you tomorrow" DeCarlos said before leaving out the door and hopping into his car. He was absolutely happy. He rolled another jay and drove home to be with Sarah.

CHAPTER 6

"Carlos wake up boy" Danielle, DeCarlos' mother said as she came through the bedroom door and opened the blinds.

As the light from the window hit his sleeping eyes he began to stir.

"Aww Ma come on five more minutes please"

"No get up we going to see your grandma today and hurry up I'm going to be downstairs fixing your breakfast"

DeCarlos took the blanket and pulled it over his head. He absolutely dreaded having to go see his grandma in the hospital.

Danielle came over and ripped the blankets off his body and tossed them to the floor leaving DeCarlos curled up in the fetal position

DeCarlos grandmother had stage four cancer and had just refused to do anymore chemotherapy.

Danielle walked to the door but before leaving she turned around and screamed.

"Get your butt up now!"

DeCarlos began to stretch and yawn before getting up and heading to the bathroom and taking care of his morning rituals as well as his hygiene.

After he is done DeCarlos walks into the kitchen and sees Sarah, his aunt Shirley, mom and dad all sitting at the table eating breakfast.

"Good morning, everyone" DeCarlos said

"Good morning" everyone said at once as they look up from eating their food.

DeCarlos walks around the table to where Sarah is sitting. Gives her a kiss and sits down next to her to begin eating his breakfast.

As DeCarlos eats his bacon, eggs, sausage, and grits he gets a strong feeling as if someone is looking at him. So, he slowly looks up and sees his dad staring right at him. He swallows his food and wipes his mouth with a napkin.

"What's wrong Dad?"

"Nothing just sitting here thinking"

"What you thinking about?"

"Your grandma, and how happy she would be to see you"

At hearing this Danielle looked up to see DeCarlos' reaction.

DeCarlos grabs his cup of orange juice and begins to gulp it down.

"Slow down DeCarlos you won't have room for your food"

"Ok Ma."

"How do you feel about seeing your grandma today DeCarlos" Bruce said

"Dad, I don't think Imma go today I have a lot of stuff to do as well as a lot of schoolwork to complete"

"Oh yeah like what?"

DeCarlos pauses for a second trying to think of something to say.

"Umm, umm, for some reason my mind is drawing a blank right now. I just know I have work to do."

Shirley looked on as DeCarlos and Bruce chatted and decided to help DeCarlos out.

"Speaking of school how was it yesterday nephew" Shirley said

"It was ok Aunt Shirley"

"What you do"

"Some stuff as we always do. A little math, a little reading and a little writing. Nothing special"

"I know it's early in the morning but boy you better give me something better than that. At least tell me what you learned yesterday."

DeCarlos went back to eating his food trying to ignore Aunt Shirley, but it didn't last long. His mother began to speak.

"Don't you hear your aunt talking to you. And I would love to know the answer myself. How about you baby"

Danielle turned to Bruce to see his reaction and let him know to play along.

"Of course I would, so what did you learn yesterday son?"

"I can't remember off hand but if I go over my notes for you it would bring back my memory. Is it ok if I go get them?"

"No that's ok son, go ahead and finish your food. We'll talk about it later. However, there is something I want to talk about with you now."

DeCarlos looks up from his food and immediately his heart drops. He's not ready for what he knows is about to come. His gut feeling is telling him his father wants to talk about Grandma.

"So DeCarlos you know we're going to see your grandma today how do you feel about seeing her?"

DeCarlos looks down at his food and begins to take his fork and play with it. All of a sudden, he feels Sarah grab his hand under the table as she gave it a quick squeeze. He looks up at her and sees her smiling. He looks into her green eyes and immediately his nervousness goes away. He's okay with talking about it now. DeCarlos turns to look at everyone else and then lays his eyes on his father. And his stomach gets butterflies.

"I don't want to talk about it Dad."

Bruce can see the look in DeCarlos' eyes begging him not to push the topic.

"It's ok we don't have to talk about it. You don't have to go either if you don't want to "

"Thanks Dad"

DeCarlos' phone rings and he picks up

"Hello"

"What's up Slim?"

DeCarlos recognizes Jeff's voice

"Coolin, what up Jeff"

"What you doing?" Jeff said.

"Eating breakfast. Why what's up"

"You trying to make some more money today?"

DeCarlos took the phone from his ear and looked at it for a second and then began talking again.

"What type of question is that of course I am. Round it off for me though"

"Around twenty-five hundred"

"I'm wit it"

"Ok, come around here when you're done"

"On my way"

DeCarlos hangs up the phone and before he gets up, he locks eyes with his dad.

"Dad may I be excused"

"Go ahead son"

DeCarlos gets up turns to speak to Sarah

"I'm about to head out you need anything Baby?"

Sarah reaches out and grabs DeCarlos' hand, looks him dead in his eyes. Her eyes give off a small sparkle as she thinks about spending time with DeCarlos.

"I would like for you to stay here with me for a little while before school starts"

"Baby, you know I would love to stay here with you but I have to meet up with Jeff before school and go over a few things. Would you like anything else?"

Sarah let go of DeCarlos' hand.

"Naw I'm good. See you when you get back from school"

"Ok Baby"

DeCarlos leaned in a gave Sarah a kiss on the forehead
"See y'all later and tell grandma I love her"
He turns quickly and heads out the door and to his car where he rolls up a jay of weed and begins smoking on the way to Jeff's house.

CHAPTER 7

DeCarlos pulls up in front of Jeff's house and calls Jeff on his cell phone. Jeff picks up after the second ring.

"Hello"

"I'm   out   front"

"Come around back"

DeCarlos gets out the car and slowly looks around at his surroundings before heading to the back yard. When DeCarlos gets around back of Jeff's house he notices Jeff cleaning one of the guns from yesterday.

"What's up Slim"

"What's up DeCarlos. About time you got here"

"Now I'm here what's up"

Jeff lets DeCarlos stand in silence as he finishes cleaning the gun. Jeff motions for DeCarlos to follow him inside the house where they both sit at a small round table.

"What's up DeCarlos"

"Money, I hope. So, tell me something good Jeff."

"You remember someone named J.B? He used to go to Douglass with us back when we were freshmen."

DeCarlos stares off into space.

"JB...JB...JB. What he look like?"

"He light-skin, about 5"4', blue eyes, he used to date Diane"

DeCarlos eyebrows shot up at the mention of Diane's name.

"You talking about sexy Diane. The one in my homeroom class"

It was complete silence for thirty seconds. DeCarlos' mind was racing trying to think of who this JB person is. Then a light bulb out on his head.

"Ooooh. You talking about JB. The one who use to drive that black car"

"Yeah!"

"I don't really know him, but I've heard of him, why?"

"Cause that's who is about to get them guns we picked up yesterday"

"Aight, what you need me to do?"

"Just drive to where I tell you to go and watch my back like you did with Angel."

"Aight I'm with it"

"Cool. Imma call JB and let him know I'm on the way."

Jeff got up and went outside to grab the bag of guns as well as his cell phone. He came back inside and dropped the big bag on the table in front of DeCarlos.

"I take it you left the gun I gave you at home right"

DeCarlos bangs a fist on the table.

"Damn! I forgot all about it. It's still in my jacket pocket at the crib."

"Well at least you know where it's. But fuck it don't trip I got you."

"Cool"

"Get one out the bag and make sure you give it back to me when we get back"

Jeff turned his back to the table and got on the phone to call JB. DeCarlos went through the bag and found a .38 snub. Put it in his pocket and sat back and waited for Jeff to get off the phone.

After about five minutes of waiting Jeff grabbed the bag and headed out the door with DeCarlos on his heels heading for the car.

"Where we headed Jeff?"

"I'll tell you when we get in the car"

Jeff and DeCarlos hopped in the car and pulled off.

"DeCarlos, you got a chocolate"

"Naw, I need to get some"

"Well in that case go to the C and A liquor store across from Madison Road Station, we can get it from there."

"Aight"

While driving down Philadelphia Ave towards Forest Heights Mall there was an uncomfortable silence. Jeff turned to DeCarlos

"What up slim. Why you so quiet?"

DeCarlos just shook his head from side to side as if he didn't want to tell Jeff what was on his mind or just couldn't find the right words to say. After a few seconds of shaking his head, he decided to talk.

"My folks going to see my grandma today. I don't know if you know but my grandma is in the hospital, and I got a bad feeling she ain't going to make it. My parents was trying to get me to go see her today, but I just can't do it"

"Why not what you worried about?" Jeff asked.

"Me and my grandma was close slim. I ain't tryna see her like that. She probably got tubes and shit coming out her body."

"How would you know if you don't go?"

"I ain't going and that's all there is to it."

DeCarlos pulls up to the C and A liquor store and gets out without saying anything. Walks into the store and gets a few packs of chocolate cigarellos and a Kiwi Strawberry Snapple and heads back to the car. As DeCarlos gets in the car he overhears Jeff on the phone.

"Meet me at the Popeyes"

As DeCarlos drives over to the Popeyes parking lot Jeff begins to twist and spark the morning jay. After taking a couple of pulls he passes the jay to DeCarlos.

DeCarlos reaches into his pocket and pulls the .38 snub out and puts it on his lap while he takes a few pulls of the jay.

"Matter a fact there goes JB right there in that black car going through the drive thru. You see him" Jeff said while pointing to the drive-thru window.

DeCarlos just shakes his head yes and passes the jay back to Jeff.

BJ pulls up on the passenger side of DeCarlos' car. Jeff rolls down the window and blows the weed smoke out.

"What up JB, what's good?"

"Shit coolin"

JB sits up in his chair to see who is sitting in the driver's seat.

"Who you got with you Jeff"

"Oh, this my mans DeCarlos he cool."

JB's left eyebrow lifted up.

"Naw Slim, you know I don't get with new motherfuckers. Hop in here with me."

"Aight" Jeff said. Before turning to DeCarlos

"Slim aim that shit at this nigga, just keep it below the window so he can't see it. If you see us scrappin' blow this nigga head off, I don't trust him at all."

DeCarlos grabs the gun off his lap.

"I got you cuz. But I ain't never shot no one before."

"Point, aim and pull the trigger it's easy"

"Aight"

DeCarlos watched as Jeff hopped in the passenger seat with the bag. And begin doing the deal.

(Ring, ring, ring) - DeCarlos' phone rang. He looked at the caller ID and the letters BM were scrolled on the screen. He picks up while still keeping his eyes and gun on Jeff.

"Hello"

"Hey baby what's up" Sarah said on the other end.

"Nothing, just chillin'. Everything ok?"

"Yeah. I found something in your coat pocket and it's really disturbing me."

"Ok, when I'm done here I'll head home so we can talk about it."

"Ok baby. Stay safe out there"

"I will, love you"

"Love you too"

He hung up the phone and noticed JB looking at him with a questionable look. JB turned to Jeff and said something, and Jeff got out of the car, gave JB a handshake and then headed inside the Popeyes. After JB pulled off DeCarlos' phone rang.

"Hello," DeCarlos Answered

"Come inside the Popeyes,"

DeCarlos put the jay out and headed inside where Jeff was at the cash register ordering some chicken and biscuits.

"You want something"

"Hell yeah. I'm hungry as shit," DeCarlos said before ordering chicken and biscuits as well. Then they stepped off to the side to have a private conversation.

"DeCarlos, I need to holla at you about something"

"What up Jeff"

"Whenever you are doing business that's not exactly legal, don't be on the phone while you're doing it."

"Why not I ain't hurting no one."

"Naw it ain't even about that. You have people who are very paranoid. I know you won't call the cops or rob me, but other people don't know that, and it can cause people to not want to deal with you or me for that matter and it's going to cost me and you money. Understand?"

DeCarlos thought a little bit before answering.

"Yeah, I do, my bad Slim. I didn't think about it like that. But now have a little dilemma."

"What's up?"

DeCarlos and Jeff moved a little closer so other people can't hear.

"Sarah found the gun in my coat pocket a few minutes ago. That's what the phone call was about earlier."

"Ok so what, she found the gun what's wrong with that?" Jeff said before shrugging his shoulders.

"Nothing is wrong with her finding the gun, it's the way she told me that has me worried. She was calm. I'm not talking about a "everything is cool", calm, it was more like a "when I see you Imma pull the trigger" calm. The only other person I know that acts like that is my mom. Whenever she is mad at my dad and people are around, she is super calm. Then when we get behind closed doors all you hear is her screaming."

DeCarlos notices the cashier pointing at them and motioning for them to pick up their food. So, he goes and gets the food and they go sit down in a booth in the corner where they can see both entrances and begin to eat. When they were done Jeff looked at DeCarlos.

"You need to handle that but not right now. And I have twenty-five hundred reasons why you should stay focused cause right now we have some more stuff to do"

"More stuff like what"

"You said you never threw a hotball at a nigga right"

"What the fuck is a hotball?"

Jeff looks at DeCarlos with wide eyes

"Are you serious DeCarlos?"

"Yeah"

Jeff lets out a huge laugh before focusing back on DeCarlos.

"Let's head to the car. I have a perfect way of explaining this to you."

When they get in the car and close the doors Jeff rolls up a jay. DeCarlos looks on as Jeff lights the weed filled blunt. After a couple of pulls Jeff passes the jay to DeCarlos. DeCarlos starts the car and pulls off, handing the jay back to Jeff.

"Good looking slim, do you think you have what it takes to put a hotball in a nigga?"

DeCarlos looks at Jeff and chuckles

"Of course I do. Don't no Kool-Aid pump in these veins."

"Oh yeah, well, do it then."

"Point him out" DeCarlos said while pulling out the .38 snub.

Jeff makes a call and starts talking

"What's up slim, I got that for you. Meet me around Arethusa Lane not too far from James Jefferson middle school." Jeff hangs up the phone and looks at DeCarlos with a cold stare.

"Head around Arethusa Lane."

DeCarlos nods

"When we get there make sure you have your hand on the trigger."

"Aight."

CHAPTER 8

About fifteen minutes later they arrive on the street.

"There he go, in the black Jeep Cherokee. Pull up next to him." Jeff said.

DeCarlos pulls up slowly and rolls the window down, gun in hand, but too low to be seen.

"What's up T?" Jeff said

"Ain't shit just tryna handle business you know," T replied.

"That's what I like to hear. Shit, follow us then."

"I'm right behind you slim."

"Pull on in the parking lot where the pond is "Jeff said and gave DeCarlos a look

before leaning in.

"DeCarlos its time to put that hotball in a nigga"

"Let's do it then"

"Aight this is what I need you to do. When I say, 'show him', I want you to drop three hot balls in him. Make sure you aim for the head, you got that

"Got ya"

"Pop the trunk"

DeCarlos pops the trunk as Jeff gets out. He watches as Jeff and T talk in front of the car. Sweat starts to build up on the hand holding the gun. His heart starts to beat fast. The sweat on his palm starts to build up so he puts the gun back in his waistband.

Then he sees Jeff walking towards his car window.

"What up Jeff"

"I want you to come introduce yourself to T, he is getting paranoid and shit."

DeCarlos gets out of the car and walks up to T with Jeff on his heels.

"What Up Slim, I'm DeCarlos"

"What's up?" The two shake hands.

"No Disrespect DeCarlos I just wanted to know who was in the car."

"It's cool T, I understand where you coming from. In this world you can never be too careful"

The words made T pause for a moment. He thought for a moment.

"You look familiar slim. Hey, hold up, your father named Bruce?"

"Yeah, why?" DeCarlos replied cautiously

"Your pops used to run wit my dad back in the day, he got pictures of them from when they used to kick it, he said his homie Bruce would always say that."

"True, he still saying that same shit?" DeCarlos said as they share a laugh.

"Well shit, I guess you just like family then slim." T said with a smile.

"No bull. Aight Jeff, he cool."

Jeff looks at them both unamused.

"Great, well I don't mean to mess up this 'family' moment, but can we talk business now, a Nigga got other stuff to do today."

"Fine nigga, damn, now whose trippin'?" T said.

"Whatever nigga, you got the money? T walks over to his car and comes back with a black duffle bag

"It's all here."

"Aight cool. Let's head to the trunk to get the stuff" Jeff said as they walk to the trunk of the car.

They open the trunk of Jeff's car.

T starts to move around the boxes in the trunk.

"There's nothing in here Jeff. What the fuck is going on"

Jeff motions for DeCarlos to step back a bit while T is distracted.

"T, why would I have them out in the open. Nigga pick up the mat and look under the spare tire."

T starts to lift up the mat as he tosses a box from one side of the trunk to the other.

"DeCarlos, he don't know what the hell he doing, *show him*."

DeCarlos walks up behind T putting the .38 to the back of his head. Before T can speak DeCarlos squeezes the trigger.

Boom, Boom, Boom

It was louder than he expected. T's body goes limp and his upper half slumps over into the trunk with his feet still touching the ground.

DeCarlos takes his free hand and wipes the blood splatter from his face. His arm still holding up the gun.

"Nigga! He bleeding all inside my trunk!"

"Hurry up Carlos, grab his legs."

DeCarlos snaps out of it.

He tosses the gun into the trunk then grabs T's legs while Jeff reaches into the trunk and grabs his arms.

Once they get a good grip, they finally lift him out of the trunk. DeCarlos stares at the blood and brain bits as they pour from the holes in T's head.

Jeff looks around scanning for a good place to dump him.

"DeCarlos, let's throw him in the woods over there."

"Aight, let's go" he agreed.

They struggle to get the body to the woods.

"Jeff let's throw him right here" DeCarlos said after a few steps into the woods.

"Hell naw, we got to put him deep in these woods cuz."

They take him further in and drop him beside a shaded area next to a fallen tree.

"Jeff help me cover him up with those leaves and sticks and stuff."

"Hold up DeCarlos. Let me check his pockets first."

Jeff goes through T's pockets grabbing his wallet and car keys.

"Aight DeCarlos, let's cover him up."

They cover the body with the leaves and shrubs lying around starting with the feet and making their way to the head and then walking out of the woods to the cars.

"Go get in your car and follow me." Jeff said.

DeCarlos runs to his car and goes to the trunk to close it. He notices the duffle bag on the ground, tosses it in the trunk and hops in the car to follow Jeff.

CHAPTER 9

After about an hour of driving, they pull up to a house that is deep in the woods. They park their cars and get out.

"Where the hell we at Jeff?" DeCarlos asks while lighting a jay.

"We at my homeboy Dee's job. He will come out in a few minutes. Help me go through this car. If you see something you want, keep it."

While Jeff is going through the trunk DeCarlos opens the glove compartment and pulls out a yellow envelope. His jaw drops as he tears it open. Inside was a brick sized stack of 100-dollar bills. DeCarlos thought to himself that it had to be well over 10 grand. He gets out quickly stuffing the envelope into his pants. Then he gets back in the truck to see what else he can find.

Just as he is about to hop back into the car a boy comes out of the house who looks to be about the same age as DeCarlos and Jeff.

"What's up Jeff"

"What up Dee!"

"What up DeCarlos?" Dee said with a smile.

"Oh, shit Dee I ain't know you lived all the way out here. Wait how the fuck are you all the way out here and still go to our school?"

Dee started laughing as he explained.

"I don't live out here, I work out here."

"What do you do then?"

"You will see soon enough. Bring the cars around back and pull them into the garage"

"Dee how much we talking?" Jeff said.

"I can give you a stack."

"Ok give it to DeCarlos."

"Aight"

"Oh, and I need you to clean out DeCarlos' trunk too. Something spilled back there."

"Knowing your ass, it's probably somebody's brains that spilled."

Jeff shrugs his shoulders and takes the jay from DeCarlos. The two get back in the cars and pull into the garage where Dee is waiting for them.

DeCarlos takes out the envelope from his pants and locks it back in the glove compartment before grabbing the duffle bag from the trunk.

"Yall go wait in the waiting area. It will be about an hour" Dee said, disappearing behind a door.

"Jeff and DeCarlos head into the house and wait in the living room on the couch.

"So, what type of place is this Jeff?" DeCarlos asks.

"It's a chop shop"

"Oh bet. What's a chop shop?"

Jeff looks at DeCarlos with one eyebrow raised.

"For your father to be who he is you sure don't know nothing about the streets"

My Dad never showed me any of this and what do you mean for 'who he is'?"

Returning the eyebrow back at Jeff.

Jeff shook his head.

"Nothin slim, nothin at all. Did you ever holla at Sarah about finding that gun in your pocket?"

"Naw, after the last phone call I never called her back to discuss it. I feel like it will be better to talk in person, you know?"

"Yeah, I understand that. How about you get her something to soften her up before you go home."

"Like what?" DeCarlos asked

"I don't know, you know your woman better than I do. Think about it."

DeCarlos laid his head back on the couch while in deep thought for the next five minutes.

"I know Sarah likes flowers."

"So, get her flowers."

"But ain't that like saying sorry, sorta? Picture this, I walk in the house with a dozen flowers, she is already pissed, what if she sees the flowers and immediately thinks 'this nigga think he slick. I see straight through him, and his bullshit ass flowers.' Next thing you know she rolling her eyes and giving me the third degree anyway."

"Damn, ok. So don't just get some regular flowers. Get them long stem red roses and go ahead and call her now. Start sweet-talking her already so by the time you go home her attitude is more mellow. You feel me?"

"Yeah, I get it, I just have to figure out everything I need to do."

DeCarlos sits back to think again. After a few moments he takes out his phone and looks at Jeff. Jeff gave him an encouraging nod and DeCarlos calls Sarah.

"Hello" she answers sharply, DeCarlos can hear the slight frustration in her voice.

"Hey beautiful"

"Hey" she replied, unphased by the compliment.

"I'm just calling to see how you and the baby doin'."

"We fine. How about you?" she asks quickly.

"I'm ok, just tryin' to make some money."

DeCarlos waited for a response, but there is only silence on the line. He tried to recover the conversation.

"I know we have not been out in a while so would you like to go out to dinner tonight?"

"Boy, we ain't got no money to be going out for dinner"

"I'm going to ask you again. Would you like to go to dinner tonight?"

After a moment of hesitation, Sarah said

"Yes"

"Ok bet, when I get home later on tonight, I want you to be dressed."

"Ok but where are we going?"

"How about Ms. Keys"

"You talking about that spot on 301, right?" her voice perks up a bit

"Yeah, that's the one"

"Ok what time do you think you will be home?"

"I'm not sure yet. It's taking me a little longer than I had expected. I will call you when I am on my way"

"Alright see you later"

"Ok baby," DeCarlos said before hanging up.

"Alright everything is set to go. I plan on taking her to Mrs. Keys"

"Yeah, I heard, that's what's up. You think that is gonna be enough to calm her down?"

"She likes the spot and all but damn, that might not be enough. Guess Imma have to get them roses too, just--" DeCarlos pauses and thinks a little bit before finishing.

"Man, fuck them roses. I really don't need them. Imma take her out and just keep it real with her.

Cause if I try to butter her up then she might look at me crazy. Then the next time I try to butter her up she is going to see straight through it."

"DeCarlos, I understand where you are coming from, but a woman likes to be treated special"

"I get it but just think about this for a little bit. I'm in love with this woman and I'm about to have a child by her. I don't want to play with her head like that. Pick her up just to let her down hard. I know she not going to like what I tell her about the gun. So, I'm not even going to play with her."

"Ok. You know your woman, so Imma stay out of it."

Just then a woman comes in from outside wearing a blue jumper and a pair of Timberland boots with a black bandana wrapped around her head.

"DeCarlos, your car is ready."

Jeff and DeCarlos get up with the duffle bag in hand and follow the woman outside to the car. Where they see Dee twisting up a jay on the hood of DeCarlos' car. They walk up on Dee in the middle of him licking the blunt and closing it.

"Which one of yall got some heat on you?" Dee said looking for a lighter to light his weed up.

"Here"

"Good looking"

"Dee, I thought it was going to take about an hour. Slim you did that quick

as shit"

"Yeah, I know. I like to get people in and out quick as possible."

Dee paused to light the jay. After he lit the jay, he opened the driver's side door and popped the trunk.

"Let me show you what I did."

Dee walked around to the trunk and DeCarlos and Jeff followed.

"Instead of cleaning it like I normally would I just gutted the whole interior of the trunk and replaced it with a new one."

"Shit, I like this one better than the old one anyway"

"What do you like about it?"

"I like the color, you know the old one was burgundy, this one is black. For some reason the black one is more soothing than the burgundy"

Dee looked at DeCarlos with a smile on his face that immediately went away.

"The only downside to the black one compared to the burgundy one is that the black one shows more blood than the burgundy. If I was y'all I think the next time you should put plastic down before you decided to…, how should I say this… make a mess!"

DeCarlos and Jeff turned to each other and just smiled. Then turned to Dee and said in unison.

"I don't know what you talking about."

Dee started to giggle a little bit and shaking his head. Then he pulled out the .38 snub.

"DeCarlos you might want this back."

"Umm yeah. I think I would like to get that back."

DeCarlos reached out and got the gun from Dee and put it in his pants pocket.

"Oh yeah DeCarlos I almost forget here"

Dee gave him the thousand dollars they agreed upon.

"Damn good looking, I did forget"

DeCarlos gave Dee a handshake and then Jeff did the same.

"Good looking on this spare of the moment type stuff Dee" Jeff said.

"It's cool, don't trip. You know for that cash, I'm there."

Dee's cell phone begins to ring.

"Hold up yall I have to get this" Dee answered the phone and stepped off.

DeCarlos, I have to make a phone call right quick." Jeff said while dialing numbers on his cell phone and stepping off to the side.

"Aight"

DeCarlos took this time to put the duffle bag in the trunk of the car.

Then he went to his glove compartment, unlocked it and took a quick peek inside to see if his package was still there. At seeing the envelope, he began to smile. Then he closed it back and hopped in the driver's side waiting to go.

Jeff hopped into the car and closed the door.

"We need to go to the motel on 201 over by Suga Hill."

"For What?"

"So, we can count and split this money. Let's wait for Dee first."

After about five minutes of waiting Dee walks over to the car.

"Hey Slim I got some business I need to handle so I'm going to need y'all to roll out."

"Aight, we got some business to handle as well so we will see you tomorrow."

Dee gave a handshake to DeCarlos and Jeff and watched them pull off.

CHAPTER 10

DeCarlos and Jeff stepped into the room with the duffle bag in tow.

"Alright DeCarlos empty the bag on the bed while I walk next door to the gas station and get some rubber bands. It's going to take about two minutes," Jeff said and walked out the door.

DeCarlos emptied the money out of the bed and his eyes immediately opened wide and his heart started beating fast. As stack by stack fell out of the bag and onto the bed. DeCarlos takes a heavy breath, and his mouth begins to water as the smell of new money enters into his nostrils. DeCarlos pauses for a few minutes just to take in the sight of all the money on the bed. Just then Jeff walks in with the pack of rubber bands, sits down on the bed and grabs a stack of money and begins to count it.

"DeCarlos, are you going to just stand there and watch me count or are you going to help?" Jeff said.

DeCarlos snaps out of his trance and realizes that Jeff came back and was sitting in front of him. DeCarlos sits down and grabs a stack of money and begins counting. An hour later the counting is over with and DeCarlos and Jeff are smoking a jay inside the room.

"Damn Jeff that's a lot of money we just counted Slim"

"That ain't a lot of money. Forty-five thousand ain't shit. Matter a fact, here"

Jeff grabs some money off the bed and tosses it to DeCarlos. Grabs the phone and walks out the door.

"I'll be back in a few minutes, got to use the phone."

"Aight"

DeCarlos takes off the rubber band and begins counting. When he's done Jeff walks in through the door and DeCarlos stands up.

"Jeff, this is only five grand. Don't get me wrong, I'm very thankful for it but don't you think I deserve half. I mean I just bodied someone for you.

47

That doesn't count for anything?"

Jeff walks over to the bed and sits down, takes a deep breath.

"DeCarlos let me explain something to you. I know you may be upset but that's just the way it is when you have a move lined up. You'll get the majority of the money. And I will get the fraction. And best believe me, in this line of work there will always be a move."

DeCarlos just stands there looking at Jeff with his hands in his pockets and thinks "there will always be a move."

"You know what, you right"

DeCarlos takes his hands out his pockets and sits on the bed.

Thinking and smoking.

"Jeff I'm hungry as shit, let's go get something to eat"

"Can't right now I got my coke connect coming through in a minute. Just sit tight. I need you to be here when he shows up. Imma show you a whole different game you can play if you want to. Imma guide you through it the same way my folks showed me.

Jeff goes to get sandwich bags and a digital scale.

But first we need to go drop that pistol off at the house. That's the easiest way to catch a bid out the feds. Getting pulled over and the police find the pistol. It don't matter if they ain't find the body yet.

Knock, Knock, Knock

DeCarlos and Jeff both turn to the door. Jeff spoke first.

"That must be my man Dom. Quick put the money in the duffle bag."

DeCarlos hurried up and put the money in the duffle bag minus his share of course. When DeCarlos was finished Jeff opened the door and in came a tall older man with dark skin, short haircut, wearing a suit and carrying a black briefcase.

"Hey Dom. What's up Slim?"

"What's up Jeff, how's my old friend doing?"

Jeff and Dom did a quick embrace.

"I'm coolin Dom. Just trying to chase that paper you know me ain't nothing change."

"That's what's up! Money make the world go round. How's school going? You are still in school right?"

"Of course I am, and it's going good still getting A's without having to study."

"That's good to hear."

Jeff closes the door and goes over to the bed.

"My apologies for being rude Dom, this is my homie DeCarlos. DeCarlos this Dom."

DeCarlos gets up and shakes Dom's hand.

"Nice to meet you sir"

"Stop it with the sir, you making me sound old. Just call me Dom. Any friend of Jeff's is a friend of mine."

"That's what's up Dom."

"Hold up you look familiar DeCarlos. Do you know someone named Bruce? He's older than ya'll probably near his forties by now. `` "

DeCarlos looks at Dom and shakes his head up and down.

"Yeah! That's my father."

"I feel sorry for you. Cause that's a crazy mother fucker there. Good man though but crazy as a mother fucker."

"Who you telling? I know from experience."

Everyone in the room broke out in fits of laughter. After the laughs stop and everyone wiped their eyes. Dom was the first to speak.

"Ok Jeff you ready to handle business?"

"Yeah, I'm ready. DeCarlos show him the money."

DeCarlos opens up the duffle bag and showed Dom the forty thousand.

"Now that's what I like to see, them dead presidents!"

"You got the product?" Jeff said.

Dom put the briefcase on the bed, popped the locks on it and opened it up, showed the product, pulled out a knife and gave it to Jeff.

"You wanna test it I hope"

"No question" Jeff said.

Jeff took the knife and poked a hole into the plastic. Took out some of the package's contents and put it on his tongue. After three seconds he felt the tip of his tongue go numb and began to shake his head up and down.

"This some good stuff! DeCarlos give him the money"

"I'm glad you like it"

Dom gets the bag and goes through it. After being satisfied with what he sees he gave Jeff and DeCarlos a handshake.

"Until next time men" Dom said as he walks out the door closing it Behind him.

DeCarlos looks on as Jeff puts the two brick like objects under the mattress. Closes the briefcase and heads to the door with the briefcase in hand.

"Come on DeCarlos I need you to stop by my house right quick so we can drop that pistol off"

DeCarlos gets up and heads to the car while Jeff locks the motel room door. Once inside the car DeCarlos takes out his pistol and puts it on his lap. Jeff hops in and off they go.

"Hey Jeff, what's in them packages?"

"What packages?"

"The packs you left at the room"

"Oh, them packs! Cocaine."

"So you took all that money and bought cocaine with it?" DeCarlos asked.

"You was there, you saw me. What are you asking me for?"

"Nothing just curious" DeCarlos said.

"Remember curiosity killed the cat"

"What the fuck is that supposed to mean?"

"You stay in this game long enough you will find out. One way or another."

DeCarlos stayed quiet the entire time at Jeff's house. Just thinking about that saying. Curiosity killed the cat. Wondering what that could have meant.

Before DeCarlos knew it he was parking the car at Jeff's house.

"Imma run this inside the crib right quick and run right back out. Then Imma need you to take me to the store down by truckers so I can get some sandwich bags. Hold up I might have a couple of boys in the house already let me check. I'll be back in a minute.

"Aight hurry up"

Jeff hops out the car and heads inside.

DeCarlos takes this time to roll up some weed and think about Sarah and his unborn child. He looks Down at the floor and notices the briefcase Jeff left. He grabs it and takes a better look at it and notices that it looks like snakeskin. He runs his hands across the briefcase in slow motion so he can capture every crack and crevice the briefcase has. Then his eyes lock on the gold dial and lock. And he wonders if it's real. Then he takes his thumbs and pulls the levers to open the briefcase. Just then the car door opens and Jeff hops in.

"You like that don't you?"

"Yeah, it's cool"

"Good it's yours. You can use it to keep all the money you made today. Just remember the combination that's already put in. Because once you turn the dial it won't open unless you put the dial on the right combination."

"Ok cool"

DeCarlos throws the briefcase in the back seat and puts the jay in the center console.

"Nigga I'm hungry as shit"

"Alright we can get some food at Arby's before we go back to the room. Hold up, let me make sure I got everything."

Jeff reaches in his pocket and grabs both boxes of sandwich bags and throws them on the floor. Then he reaches into another pocket and gets both digital scales and throws them on the floor as well.

"Food has to be on you, I just put my money in the house. That cool?" Jeff said.

"I got you"

DeCarlos pulls off and heads to the Arby's where they order a lot of food. Then head down the street to the motel. Jeff and DeCarlos go in the room, sit on the bed and eat their food. After they get finished, they begin to handle business.

"Ok DeCarlos Don't throw them bags away cause we going to need them. And dry out two of them cups. Good, I mean real good."

DeCarlos went to go do his part.

Jeff took two sandwich wrappers and spread them across the table and emptied half of the cocaine out of the first package.

By time Jeff was done emptying the half, DeCarlos was back in the room with the two cups. Sat down beside Jeff and watched in complete awe.

"DeCarlos, how many grams are in an ounce?"

"What the fuck you asking me that question for?"

"Nigga answer the question"

DeCarlos begins to think then it comes to him.

"28 why?"

"Alright I need you to get a cup and a sandwich bag then put the sandwich bags on the digital scale and scoop the coke into the sandwich bag until the scale reads 28.0 then tie the sandwich bag and put it in the Arby's bag. Only put nine bags in one Arby's bag. Watch. Do it like this."

Jeff showed him what to do and then DeCarlos started doing it himself. They were in there for about an hour and a half bagging up ounces of cocaine. When they finished, they grabbed the Arby's bag and got into the car.

"DeCarlos, I need you to hold on to four of these bags. Here put them in the briefcase.

DeCarlos wraps them up and puts them in the briefcase.

"Alright. Drop me off at the house. I'll see you tomorrow at school."

On the way to the house his phone rings. He picks up without looking at the caller ID.

"Hello?"

"Hey baby you on your way home yet?" Sarah said.

"It's funny you should ask that because I just dropped Jeff off and now, I'm in the car about five minutes away from the house. You dressed?"

"Yeah, I'm dressed"

"What you got on?"

DeCarlos could hear Sarah laughing on the other end of the phone.

"Boy it's not time for that. Cause my stomach is hurting and I'm starving.

"So, what you saying is that after we eat you going to make yourself my dessert"

"Maybe. Why you go a sweet tooth"

Now it was DeCarlos' turn to laugh.

"Of course I do. The crazy thing is I have had one all day and guess what."

"What?"

"It's only for you."

"Boy please. You must think you're smooth or something. Hurry your butt on home, I'm hungry." Sarah hangs up the phone.

DeCarlos looks at his cell phone as if it made him confused. And then more to himself than to anyone else he said.

"Mood swings are a bitch"

After he parks the car in front of the house he takes his money out, counts it and puts it in the briefcase. Then heads inside and up to the room to wash up and change. When he's done, he calls for Sarah.

"Sarah, I'm ready."

Sarah comes into the room with the briefcase in one hand and the gun in the other. And sets them on the bed.

"DeCarlos I can't wait, I need to talk to you about this now." Sarah said while pointing at the gun.

"And by the way what's in the briefcase?"

DeCarlos looks down at the briefcase and walks over to the bed and sits down. Grabs Sarah's hand and motions for her to sit next to him.

"The gun was for protection. I was going somewhere with Jeff, and he asked me to hold it for him just in case something went wrong. And I forgot to give it back to him, that's all. And he said I could keep it when I asked him if he wanted it back."

"Keep it for what?"

"To protect ourselves"

"Protect us from what?"

"Thieves and robbers"

"Now you definitely not making any sense. We don't have anything for them. Even if some did want to rob us."

"We didn't at first, now we do"

DeCarlos opened up the briefcase and took out the six thousand and gave it to Sarah. Then took out the yellow envelope and emptied it on the bed.

Sarah's green eyes opened wider than DeCarlos had ever seen. She grabbed at some of the money and began to smell it.

"Sarah, I want to spend my life with you, and I want to make our lives comfortable. That way we don't have to stress about a lot of things."

Sarah reached out her arms with wads of money in each hand, grabbed DeCarlos and gave him a big hug.

"Oh baby I love you so much"

"I love you too baby."

"Now let's go hurry up and eat so I can have my dessert."

Sarah starts to giggle and then said.

"Boy you stupid" With a big smile on her face.

CHAPTER 11

April 21 (three months later)

"What's up DeCarlos?" Jeff asked.

"Shit coolin, waiting for Sarah to get out the shower so I can say my goodbyes and make my rounds" DeCarlos said to Jeff as he sits on the bed watching TV and talking on his cell phone.

"Who are you going to see first?"

"Remember that chick that was working the cash register at Popeyes that was on my line a couple months ago"

"Yeah, I remember her. Why what's up?"

"Well she hit me last week just wanting to talk. Next thing I know she asked me if I knew where to find a little bit of this and a little bit of that. I said maybe, maybe not, how about you let me come over so we can talk in person. We set a date and it just so happens that today is the day."

DeCarlos started flipping through channels some more.

"You going to fuck her ain't you?" Jeff asked.

"Hell naw I ain't going to fuck that bitch. Is you crazy?"

"Fuck what bitch" Sarah said as she gets out the shower and walks across the room.

"Just some bitch that wants me to come over and introduce her to a few new things."

Sarah stops in her tracks, belly about to burst with her hands on her hips.

"You better not be introducing no things to her at all" gesturing to her very pregnant belly.

After saying this Sarah looks down at DeCarlos' crotch.

"And I mean no things!"

DeCarlos could hear Jeff on the other end of the phone laughing and repeating her.

"And I mean no things" Jeff mocked.

"Nigga shut up" DeCarlos said.

"Boy who the fuck you telling to shut up!" Sarah screams at DeCarlos as she puts the coco butter on her stomach.

"This asshole on the phone!"

"Heeeey Sarah," Jeff said from the other end of the phone.

DeCarlos volume on his cell phone must have been on high because Sarah replied as if she heard him clear as day.

"Hey Jeff. You better not be getting my man into no shit you hear me?"

"Yeah, I hear you"

"You better"

"Hey DeCarlos" Jeff said.

"What's up?"

"I'm bout to get off this phone, handle that and call me when you're done."

"Aight," DeCarlos said as he hung up the phone. Got off the bed and kissed Sarah and walked out the front door.

As soon as DeCarlos gets in his car his phone rings.

"Hello?"

"Hey DeCarlos, it's Erika."

"Hey beautiful. How's it going?"

"I'm good and you?"

"I'm maintaining, chasing money as usual. Speaking of money, tell me something to make me smile."

"I don't have on any panties and my pussy wet as shit" she said lowering her voice.

At hearing this DeCarlos puts on a huge smirk.

"Did that make you smile, DeCarlos?" Erika asked knowing that it did.

DeCarlos turns on his serious tone, "no, not at all."

"Well how about it I tell you I want you to stick that dick inside this pussy and let me cum all over it. Then I want you to shove it in my mouth so I can see what I taste like."

DeCarlos begins to move his leg back and forth as he sits in the driver's seat. Trying not to get too excited.

"Damn girl, you got my dick hard as shit. You going to make me come over there and do something real big with you if you don't stop talking like that."

"You know I can put my legs behind my head, right?" Erika said with a playful tone.

DeCarlos puts the key in the ignition and starts the car up. Then he remembers he forgot something inside.

"Erika don't get me wrong I would love to come out there and make you cum. But shorty, I'm about my money and I ain't about to come all the way out there for nothing less than three hundred. So unless you spending three or better. Imma have to move on."

"I ain't got no problem spending that. By time I get back from the bank you should be getting close right?"

DeCarlos gets out the car and heads back inside.

"Call you when I'm out front."

"Ok Baby," DeCarlos replied and hangs up the phone.

He goes to his room and looks under the bed and grabs the briefcase, opens it and gets one of the ounce bags out along with the digital scale and runs back to the car. Gets in and speeds off. Headed towards Erika's house.

Forty-five minutes later DeCarlos is parking down the street from where Erika lives before putting the car in park DeCarlos makes sure he can see the front of Erika's house. He takes his phone out and calls Erika.

"Hello."

"Hey Erika."

"Where you at?"

"I'm about seven to eight minutes away."

Ok. The door will be open, just come inside."

"Aight see you in a few."

"Ok" Erika said as DeCarlos hung up the phone.

DeCarlos sat in his car for the next five minutes watching who come out of Erika's house. He noticed three guys come out with beer in their hands, hop in a car and leave.

After they left, he called Erika back.

"Hello" She answered.

"Hey Erika. I'm out front, come to the car and bring that with you." DeCarlos said quickly as he pulled up in front of Erika's house then hung up the phone.

A couple of seconds later Erika comes out the house with a red robe on and some Tweety bird slippers. Walks quickly to the car and gets in.

"Hey baby. I thought you was going to come inside." Erika said in a sweet voice while turning her body to be able to face DeCarlos.

"Yeah, I was but I ended up getting a business call."

"Oh, okay."

"Give it here,"

Erika's eyebrows went low as if she was confused.

"The money Erika" DeCarlos explained.

Erika reached in her robe and took out the three hundred and gave it to DeCarlos.

"Here Baby." As he took the money Erika's smile dropped.

"Don't act like that, remember what I told you, business first. Business first."

DeCarlos reached over and opened the glove compartment to get a sandwich bag and let his hand slide across Erika's thigh.

Here robe slipped off her thighs and fell on the seat.

DeCarlos then tapped the inside of her thigh so she could open her legs so he could reach down and get a scale and the bag of cocaine from off the floor. After getting the scale and bag he took out some cocaine and put it in the empty bag and weighed it.

"3.5 on the nose. Damn I'm good" DeCarlos said as he gave it Erika"

"You gone to see what your money bought Erika?"

"Of course I am. It's just that whenever I get high, I want to fuck."

"Is that right? I'm pretty sure we can work something out."

DeCarlos reaches over and begins to rub Erika's bare thigh which puts a smile on Erika's face.

"First, why don't you go ahead and get your mind right."

"You sure it's going to be okay?" Erika asked with puppy dog eyes.

"Listen Erika. I want you to be comfortable." DeCarlos' hand went further up her thigh. DeCarlos looked Erika in her eyes.

"There's nothing wrong with you if you get your mind right every once in a while. Your secret is safe with me. I won't tell anyone as long as you don't either."

DeCarlos' hand went even higher up her thigh. His pinky finger rubbed the pubic hairs on her pussy. And he felt the heat coming from it.

Erika shook her head up and down and grabbed the bag with the coke in it. Stuck her thumb nail in it and put the contents to her nose and snorted it up in one snort. Tilted her head back and waited for the drain to drip into her throat.

"Open your legs wide," DeCarlos said, knowing what was about to happen.

Erika put one leg in DeCarlos' lap and the other out the window.

DeCarlos could hear her start to moan from the cocaine starting to work. So he stuck his fingers in her pussy and immediately she gasped. He worked his finger in and out slowly saving the sight of her inner pussy lips opening and closing. As his fingers began to get wetter, he noticed Erika's eyes were closed and she was biting on her bottom lip.

"You want me to go deeper?" DeCarlos said with his dick starting to stiffen.

"Oh yes. Go Deeper, please go deeper!" Erika begged DeCarlos while moving her hips up and down.

DeCarlos opens Erika's robes and grabs onto her nipple and begins to pluck it. Not hard enough to hurt but not soft enough to not be felt. Then he puts his fingers in deeper and begins to move them in and out a little faster. Just enough to match her hip thrust. Every time her hips come up; he goes a little deeper. Erika looks over and sees DeCarlos' dick print and grabs it and begins to rub it through his pants.

"You want this dick don't you" DeCarlos said while looking Erika in the eyes.

All she could do was shake her head up and down in between moans.

"I want you to come all over these fingers first. Then we'll talk about it."

DeCarlos reaches over Erika and pulls the lever to reline her chair. The chair falls back with a thud. (bang)

But DeCarlos fingers never stop. Now they are soaking wet from Erika's pussy juice. DeCarlos picks up speed and depth now that his angle is better. He takes a peek at his fingers, and he can see the juice flying off and landing on her inner thighs. So he grabs a titty and starts messaging it. Instantly her moans become "Oh shits", and her legs start to shake quickly, and she squeezes his dick. He starts to massage her titty a little rougher and fingers her pussy deeper and deeper until he can't go any further.

Then she screams, "I'm about to cum! I'm about to cum!"

Erika grabs the back of the head rest with both hands, closes her eyes tight and takes a deep breath. And shouts.

"I'm cumming." Erika lifts her waist up and comes all over DeCarlos' fingers. He has cum dripping down his forearm and onto the floor.

"Damn girl you gotta waterfall in between those legs."

Erika sits up and goes straight for DeCarlos' dick and starts unbuttoning his pants.

"Now you see what I got, let me taste what you got." Erika said before she puts DeCarlos' dick in her mouth.

"Shit handle your business. Matter a fact, before you see what I taste like, clean my fingers off."

Erika grabs DeCarlos' fingers and licks them clean. While looking DeCarlos in his eyes.

"What they taste like."

"Heaven?"

DeCarlos began to think about the men who came out of her house before he got there.

"I'm not ready to die yet so I'll let heaven wait."

"When you ready to go let me know" Erika replied.

"I'm ready to go to one particular place right now"

"Oh yeah, where?" Erika said with a little attitude.

DeCarlos reaches out and grabs the back of Erika's neck and pushes her head down onto his dick.

"Home" DeCarlos said as he tilts his head back and enjoys the feeling of Erika's warm mouth wrapped around his dick.

For the next 10 minutes Erika sucks, slurps, and moans on DeCarlos' dick. She deepthroats DeCarlos as he shoots his load into her mouth, and she swallows every bit of it.

"You want to take this inside DeCarlos?"

"Naw Imma need to handle the business from earlier."

"Okay Baby, hit me later" Erika said as she got out the car and went into the house. DeCarlos zips up his pants and takes out his phone to call Jeff.

Ring, Ring, Ring

Jeff picks up on the other end. "What up cuz?

CHAPTER 12

DeCarlos begins to head back to his house, "Ain't shit coolin. Tryna make some more money before Sarah hits my phone talking about, she wants some food."

"Ain't she 9 months pregnant?"

"Yeah. So you know I'm tryna get this money so I can do what I need to do as a father." DeCarlos said as he looked in the rearview mirror while driving down the street.

He notices a black Lincoln Navigator a few cars back that doesn't sit well with him. So he decides to keep his eyes on it.

"Yeah, I can understand you, fatherhood must come with a lot of responsibility. So check this out. I just got a call a couple minutes ago from one of my old friends. I need you to go pick up a bulldog for me." Jeff said.

DeCarlos makes a right turn at a light and looks in his mirror to see if the black car makes the turn with him.

"You want to get a dog?" DeCarlos said as he sees the car pull around the corner. DeCarlos makes a left turn this time and parks at the first house he comes across. And gets low in his driver's seat. Fixes the mirror so he can see behind him. To see if the car actually follows.

"You'll see when you pick it up. It's not too far from Ms. K's I'll text you the address."

"Aight" DeCarlos said as he hangs up the phone and sees the Navigator roll slowly pass. Trying to peek into his car. He notices a dark-skinned male with short hair in the passenger side window. DeCarlos stored the face in his memory bank and waited for the car to get a block away before he pulls away from the house. As he's driving down the street, he gets a text on his phone. With the address of the pick-up. And calls Jeff back.

"Hello," Jeff said.

"I got it. I'm right around the corner from it." DeCarlos said as he made the correct turns to lead him to the house.

"Good cause they expecting you. Knock on the door and ask for the twins. Make sure you ask for the twins."

"Aight. I'm here right now I'll see you back at the house"

"Ok," Jeff said.

DeCarlos gets out the car and notices the black Navigator pull in and try to hide behind a dumpster. He plays it off as if he doesn't see it. He walks up the driveway to the front door and knocks. A dark skin girl opens up the door.

"Hello," she said.

"The Twins here?"

"Yeah. Come inside and have a seat. They'll be out in a second"

"Ok"

DeCarlos walks in the house and sits on the couch. Takes out his phone and hits the redial button.

Ring, Ring, Ring, Ring, Ring

"Everything ok?"

"Naw not really Bruh! I got this black Navigator that followed me all the way from shawty house. I tried to shake them back around her way. I thought I did but I seen them pullin up behind a dumpster. Right before I walked in."

"Are they still there?"

"Hold up, let me see," DeCarlos said as he got up off the couch and went over to the window. He slid the curtain back just a little, just enough to peek out. And saw them still there but from his angle he could see them both now.

"Yeah, they still there. They got the window rolled down and smoking a jay"

"Can you see they faces?" Jeff asked.

"Yeah"

"Tell me what they look like"

"The driver is dark skinned as well as the passenger. The driver has long red dreads with blue tips and the passenger has short hair," DeCarlos left the window and sat down on the couch.

"As soon as you said red dreads with blue tips I was lost. I don't know who that is. You get to see the twins yet? Jeff said

"Naw the chick said they going to be out in a second"

"Ok when the twins get there hand the phone to whoever you see" DeCarlos sees the girl walking towards him with something in her hand.

"Matter a fact here comes the chick right now"

"Give her the phone"

The girl gave DeCarlos a brown shoe box. And gave her the phone.

"Someone needs to talk to you" DeCarlos said to the dark-skinned girl.

She takes the phone and begins to talk. She walks over to the same window DeCarlos was at and peeks out. Says a few more words and walks away from the window into a back room.

DeCarlos opens the box and sees two 44 Bulldogs in it, that look exactly the same.

"The twins" DeCarlos whispers to himself.

Just then the girl comes back out with a book bag in one hand and two thirty shot, Glock nines in the other. She sits the bookbag down next to him and gave him the guns. She reaches in her back pocket and hands him the phone.

"Hello," DeCarlos said.

"Nobody knows them, so you got to take care of it. Be smart and quick, see you when you get here." Jeff hangs up the phone. DeCarlos takes the book bag and puts the box inside as well as the phone.

Throws the bookbag on and grabs the guns. He cocks them back to make sure there's a bullet in the chamber. Goes back to the window and peeks out.

"You got a back way out of here" DeCarlos asks the girl.

"Yeah, follow me."

She walks through the house until she gets to a stairwell.

She points.

"Down the steps and first door on the left will lead you to the back yard."

"Thanks" DeCarlos said as he raced down the steps and out the back door. He comes to a big fence that keeps him out the neighbor's yard. So he tucks both guns into his waistband and begins to climb over. Once over he runs across two yards and once he gets to the third one he walks slowly to the front yard to see where the black car is. DeCarlos peaks around the bricks of the house and sees the car at the corner of the front yard. He kneels down and takes out both guns and begins to creep up on the car from behind. The two people inside were too busy smoking and looking straight ahead that they didn't see DeCarlos coming. DeCarlos could hear them talking and smell the weed. He was so close. He raised both his guns to the passenger's temple and let the bullets fly through the open window. \

Bang, bang, bang, bang, bang, bang, bang, bang

With each squeeze of the trigger bullets ripped through the faces and necks of both the passenger and driver. Blood squirted over the dashboard and windshield and onto his face. Their bodies jerked back and forth. As each slug hits its mark. DeCarlos stopped shooting. He noticed the passenger leaned over into the driver and the driver leaned up against the door, their faces unrecognizable. DeCarlos ran to his car and jumped in thru the guns on the seat next to him. Started the car up and sped off.

A few minutes later DeCarlos arrives at Jeff's house and knocks on the front door. After about a minute of waiting DeCarlos goes around the backyard where he sees Jeff and Angel.

Jeff is on the grill barbequing and drinking a beer and Angel is standing next to him looking at the ribs being glazed.

DeCarlos looks at Angel and immediately starts to feel butterflies in his stomach. She was stunning. She wore her long hair up in a bun. And had on a blue halter top, nipples super hard, looking like gumdrops. With white stretch pants and blue and white reeboks on. She smiled at him, and he smiled back then he went over to the cooler and grabbed a beer, opened it and began to chug. Jeff walks over and begins to talk to DeCarlos.

"Damn Slim, slow down, you going to get brain freeze"

DeCarlos pays Jeff no attention and keeps chugging.

Jeff looks over to Angel.

"His adrenalin must still be going after the work he put in."

DeCarlos stops drinking.

"Yeah, that's it. What was the first time you put in work?" Angel said as she walked over to DeCarlos locking eyes with him.

"No that ain't the first time." DeCarlos paused for a second.

"Hold up. How ya'll know about it already? It just happened less than thirty minutes ago." DeCarlos said, looking back and forth between both Angel and Jeff.

Jeff walked back over to the grill and began to flip them.

"I called the twins' mother back and she told me. She didn't tell me the details though I figured I would get them from you. You got the twins right" Jeff asked.

"Yeah, they right here." DeCarlos took off the bookbag and took out the smashed shoe box.

"There you go Angel, the twins you were looking for."

"Aight Jeff. Let me go through these in the car and I will come right back." Angel said as she grabbed the shoe box from DeCarlos and headed to her car.

DeCarlos' eyes was glued to her butt as she walked.

"Damn I didn't know she was that phat."

"Yeah, she most certainly is" Jeff laughed a little.

"How about you tell me about the work you put in today."

"Ain't too much to talk about really. I had a problem and I dealt with it. DeCarlos said as he went over to get a plate of food.

 Jeff just watched him as he grabbed his food.

"I should have known better than to ask you about work. Even the first time you didn't really talk about it. Why not?"

DeCarlos just shrugged his shoulders and took a bite out of the ribs that he just got.

Just then Angel comes back and sits next to DeCarlos, grabs his beer and takes a swig of it. DeCarlos looks at Jeff and continues his conversation with him.

"Because sometimes what's already understood doesn't need to be explained." Jeff looks at DeCarlos and shakes his head up and down slowly as in a silent agreement. Angel looks on in confusion. As silence overcomes the three of them. Angel takes another drink of the beer and then gave out a hug belch.

"Ok what yall talking about and why y'all so damn quiet?"

DeCarlos was the first to respond, "I was just telling Jeff that I don't need to explain what happened because what's already understood doesn't need to be explained you know."

Angel understood what DeCarlos was saying so she took out some weed and a blunt and began rolling a jay.

The three of them finished smoking, ate and enjoyed each other's company for a few hours. DeCarlos sits in the lawn chair with a beer in his hand. Angel sits in the same lawn chair facing DeCarlos; they both pass a jay back and forth and are deep in conversation. While Jeff is in the house.

"DeCarlos, is it okay if I ask some personal questions? Angel asks while looking DeCarlos in the eyes. DeCarlos takes a drink and a puff of the jay. And then responds.

"Yeah, what's up?"

"I was asking Jeff about you, and he said you have a kid on the way and you're still with your soon to be baby's mother, is that true?"

"Damn I wish he wouldn't be talking about my personal business... but yeah, it's true" DeCarlos passes the weed to Angel. Angel takes the jay, leans forward and places her hand on DeCarlos' upper thigh.

"Do you love her?"

"No question" Angel removes her hand and sits up straight, takes a few pulls of the jay and passes it back to DeCarlos.

"I wonder what it's like to be loved."

DeCarlos gets up out the chair, stretches and looks at his watch.

"It's time for me to go, I need to go check up on my girl."

DeCarlos reaches down and gave Angel a hug.

"There is someone out there that can love you the way you deserve to be loved but that love starts with honest friendship."

They cut their embrace short, and Angel stands up.

"We're friends aren't we DeCarlos."

DeCarlos pulls out his cell phone and gave it to her and smiled.

"Not until you put your number in that phone."

Angel looks at DeCarlos and sees the message in his eyes which makes her smile. She put her number in his phone and then called her phone so she can have his and then gave the phone back. DeCarlos begins to walk away and then turns to Angel.

"Maybe one day I can show you," DeCarlos said loudly.

A confused look comes across Angel's face.

"Show me what?"

"What it feels like to be loved" Feeling tired and a little tipsy DeCarlos gets in the car and heads home.

The whole way home he was on cloud nine all he could think about was Angel and how it would feel to love her.

His phone begins to vibrate so he takes it out and answers it without looking at the caller ID.

"Hello"

"DeCarlos" The voice said on the other end.

"Hey ma everything ok?"

"Yeah? Why?"

"Talk to you when you get here"

The phone hung up. DeCarlos looked at the phone as if it just cussed him out.

"What the fuck was that about," he said aloud and continued home.

CHAPTER 13

DeCarlos walks into the kitchen and sees the briefcase that was supposed to be upstairs sitting on the table. He opens it and finds it empty. No money, no cocaine, and no gun. DeCarlos' heart drops into his stomach. He takes off up the steps to his room. Sarah's gone, the TVs on, the bed's made up and it smells like perfume. Then she hears the toilet flush over and over and over again. He rushes to the bather and sees his mother leaned over the toilet. He sees the bathtub faucet running on high.

"Ma, what you doing?"

"What it look like I'm doing?"

DeCarlos looks a little closer and notices his mother popping bags and pouring its white contents in the toilet and flushing it. Then he looks into the bathtub and notices the popped bags and Arby's bags floating in the water.

DeCarlos tries to grab the bag out of his mom's hand, and she pushes him hard to the floor. Looks him in the eyes.

"Boy you not going to go down this route. You not going to put my life in jeopardy. I done worked too fuckin hard for what we got. Nigga is you fuckin stupid" Danielle said while putting her finger in DeCarlos' face and jabbing him in the forehead with it.

"Your dad put me through hell dealing with this shit and I'm not going through it again. Do you understand me?"

"Yes ma'am" DeCarlos said as he got up off the floor and went outside to his car. He got in and pulled off around the corner, rolled up a jay and began to spark it. He pulled out his cell and called Jeff.

"Hello"

"We got a little problem."

"What's up cuz"

DeCarlos pulled off and headed to the pond where he dropped his first body.

"My mom found the stash and got rid of it"

"Well you know you owe me what was left, plus interest. It shouldn't be a problem though. You stashed the money away, right?"

"She got that too"

"Well then, you might just have a little problem. Call me when you get it. You got 72 hours." Jeff hung up the phone.

DeCarlos pulled into the parking lot and just sat there thinking and smoking. He had to find out what to do next. So he pulled out his cell phone and dialed his father's number.

"Hey son," Bruce said when he picked up.

"Hey dad, where you at?"

"I'm at work over here on Main Street. Everything ok?"

"You heard from ma?"

"No."

"I need to talk to you now, it's important."

"Well bring your ass on up here and stop wasting my minutes."

"On my way."

DeCarlos hung up the phone and headed to his father's job. Ten minutes later DeCarlos pulled up and parked. He noticed his father out front smoking a cigarette. Which he doesn't do unless something is bothering him. DeCarlos beeps the horn twice to let his dad know he's there. Bruce walks over to the car and gets in.

"Hey son"

"Hey Dad"

"You smell like weed. You got some left?"

DeCarlos reaches in the ashtray and pulls out a half of jay and gave it to his father.

"Thanks son, I need this"

"As soon as I got off the phone with you, I decided to call your mom to find out what's going on. And she told me everything." Bruce lit the jay, inhaled deeply and then blew the smoke out.

"How much you owe this person."

DeCarlos grabbed the jay from his dad and took a few pulls.

"More than I can afford."

"Do you know the people this person does business with? Because that's how we going to get the money. How long do you have to pay it?"

"72 hours." DeCarlos replied

"Well I guess we should go ahead and get started then let me clock out and then we can put a game plan together. In the meantime come inside and say hi to your aunts and granddad." Bruce gets out the car and heads inside with DeCarlos on his heels. Right before going inside Bruce turns to DeCarlos.

"Matter a fact who is this person you owe"

"Jeff"

"Your best friend?"

"Yeah"

"Shit why don't we just kill the little fuck and get it over with."

"We can't"

Bruce understood what his son meant by "can't". It wasn't that Jeff couldn't be touched; it was because they were friends.

"Ok"

Bruce and DeCarlos walked into the restaurant while Bruce went to the back to clock out. DeCarlos hung out with his aunt's and granddad for a few minutes and did some catching up. When Bruce returned, they left and stood outside DeCarlos' car.

"DeCarlos the only reason I'm helping you is because I love you."

"I know Dad" DeCarlos said while looking down at his foot while he rolled a few pebbles under his sole.

"DeCarlos look at me"

DeCarlos raised his head slowly and made eye contact with his father.

"DeCarlos, you have to promise me after all this is over. You will leave this game alone and focus on school and Sarah. Deal?"

Bruce held out his hand waiting from the handshake he knew would come. DeCarlos looked at the hand in front of him and grabbed it in a firm grip.

"Deal"

"Ok son. First order of business, you got a strap?"

"Naw Ma took it when she took the coke"

"She never mentioned a gun when I talked to her."

"Well that's where it was"

"Don't worry I got you"

"Meet me at Tuckers in 30 minutes" Bruce said and then headed to his car. Leaving DeCarlos with a smile on his face.

CHAPTER 14

Thirty minutes later DeCarlos pulls into the parking lot of the Truckers restaurant. And sees his father sitting with the car door open and smoking a cigarette. So he pulls up next to Bruce.

"Dad what's up"

Bruce raises his head and sees his son. Reaches over to the passenger seat and grabs a brown paper bag, flat head screwdriver and two license plates. Gets out and shuts the door. And throws the bag into DeCarlos' lap and proceeds to take off DeCarlos' license plates and put on the ones he brought with him. DeCarlos takes a peek in the bag and notices an old rusty .38 long. He closes the bag and puts it in the seat next to him. Bruce hops in the car and throws the flat head on the floor of the car as well as the plates.

"Ok where we headed."

"I don't know" DeCarlos said

Bruce looked at DeCarlos with a puzzled look

"I thought you said you knew some of his people"

"I do"

"Ok. So take me to who needs to get it first" Bruce said as he leaned back in the chair and closed his eyes.

"Wake me up when we get there son."

As DeCarlos put the car in gear and pulled off he responds, "I got you Dad". The car was completely silent the whole ride to New Carlton Station. Once there DeCarlos pulled into the same spot he was in last time, parked and looked around to see if he could spot John. No more than 15 seconds went by before DeCarlos' eyes landed on his target. DeCarlos tapped his dad on the arm to wake him up.

"Dad, Dad, wake up. There go that nigga right there."

Bruce took off his hat, wiped his face and tried to focus. "Where he at?"

"He the nigga leaning up against the bus stop. With the red Cubs hat on.

You see him?" Bruce took a few seconds to look at all the bus stops and then he spots him.

"Yeah, I got him. How you know him?"

"When I first started, we came through here and Jeff dropped a package off to him." Bruce turned to DeCarlos.

"What was the package?"

"Don't know."

Bruce turned back to look at John and noticed him walking over to a gray Ford Taurus.

"What ya'll do while ya'll was here, did y'all smoke?" Bruce said with his eyes still glued to John. John took something out his pockets, put it in a brown paper bag and threw it under the car and walked back over to the bus stop.

"Nothing, just smoke" DeCarlos said.

"Did you share a jay or did he spark his own?"

"His own."

"Ok this what I need you to do. Go over there and tell him you need to buy some tree. And get him in the car, got it?"

"Yeah Dad, I got it."

Bruce got the bag with the gun in it. Took it out and put it on the side of the door.

DeCarlos got out and walked up to John. "What's up John"

"What's up DeCarlos"

"How's life treating you?"

"Shitty, that's why I'm out here tryna get this money"

John said while looking around for regular customers.

"I feel you. But check this out, you got some tree you tryna sell?"

"Always" John reached in his pocket.

"Naw not here in the open. Come to the car." Before John could disagree DeCarlos was walking towards his car. John needed the money bad, so he followed. Once in the car DeCarlos turned to John.

"How much can I buy?"

"I only have dub bags. How many you need?" Then John noticed Bruce in the front seat and gave DeCarlos a suspect look. DeCarlos picked up on it.

"Damn my fault. This is my dad, Dad this is John."

Bruce gave John a head nod and John returned it.

"Ok, now that that's out of the way, can I get high?" John reached in his pocket and pulled out a sandwich bag full of weed in little baggies. When he looked up to ask DeCarlos how many he needed he saw Bruce with a gun in his hand and it was pointed directly at his head.

"Ok John, this ain't personal, just business. Now strip!" Bruce said in a deep voice. John looked over at DeCarlos with pleading eyes. DeCarlos looked from John to the gun and back at John.

"I'm not the one with the gun cuz. He is."

John reluctantly begins to take off his clothes.

"Put everything in your pockets on the seat next to you" Bruce said before turning to DeCarlos but making sure the gun was still on Jeff.

"DeCarlos, you see that gray Ford Taurus over there in the corner of the parking lot?"

DeCarlos looked over the head rest and out the back window into the corner of the parking lot.

"Yeah, I see it, why?"

"There is a brown paper bag under the car go get it"

DeCarlos did as instructed and went over to the cat and looked under it. There were three brown bags and DeCarlos grabbed them all and headed back to the car. When he got in John was putting his clothes back on.

"If you tell the cops we gonna come back and kill you, you understand?" Bruce said quickly.

"Yeah, I got you" John said. With his feelings a little hurt.

"Aight get out and don't slam the door son."

John got out, fixed his clothes and walked off as DeCarlos put the car in gear and pulled off.

Bruce turns to DeCarlos before getting the bags and opening them.

"How much you think we got?"

"I don't know Dad. Check the bags "Bruce opens the bags and empties each one into his lap. Two of the bags contain weed while the other contains small unorganized bills. While DeCarlos Drives Bruce counts the money. Once he is done, he turns to DeCarlos.

"You got fifteen hundred in these bags. Is that enough?"

"Nowhere near it pops"

"Well we are going to have to get someone who is heavier in the game. I have a few people I know from back in the day, but I consider them friends so that's a no go. Do you know someone?" Bruce said while leaning back in his chair.

"I know someone who is pretty deep. His name is Dee, he runs a chop shop."

"What else you know about him?"

"I go to school with him and that's about it. Imma make a few phone calls once we get back home to try to find out more."

"Aight well in that case, wake me up when we get back to tuckers." Bruce closes his eyes and prepares to drift off to sleep. For the rest of the ride DeCarlos is silent and lost in thought. Twenty minutes later DeCarlos pulls into the restaurant next to his father's car. He gets the plates and the flat head from under Bruce's feet, gets out and proceeds to change the plates back to the original ones. When he is finished, he gets in the car and taps Bruce on the shoulder "Dad, Dad get up."

"What's up?"

"We at your car and here is the plates"

DeCarlos hands the plates to Bruce who looks at them with a quick glance.

"Aight, I'm gone home, see you when you get there. We can talk about the rest after breakfast tomorrow". Bruce gets out the car, shuts the door and leans in the window. "Don't tell Ma about this; no matter what she said." DeCarlos shakes his head up and down

"I got you."

"Aight."

Bruce hits the hood of the car two times and steps off to get in his car. DeCarlos watches and then pulls off. Headed home.

"Hey Dad, hey ma" DeCarlos said as he pulls out the chair at the kitchen table and sits down.

"Hey DeCarlos" Danielle said as she leans over the table and puts a bowl of string beans and some plates on it. Bruce looks at his wife's butt as she bends over the table

"It looks just as good as the first day we met," Bruce said with a smile on his face, reaching out and softly tapped her butt. Danielle looks back at Bruce

"I know. It's all them squats I do that still got me looking like I'm 18."

Then she sits down so they can begin to eat. Bruce looks over at DeCarlos and gave him a head nod.

"What's up Son, everything good?"

DeCarlos looks at Bruce with a smile on his face and laughter in his eyes.

"I know that look DeCarlos. What's so funny" Bruce said.

DeCarlos begins to laugh and point at his mom and dad. "Yall are. Yall acting like your teenagers. And y'all don't do that too often, that's what is so funny. It's just good to see"

"Well that's because we're in a good mood this morning. And every day Jehovah allows us to wake up is a blessing so we should enjoy it. You understand what I'm saying son?"

"Yeah, I understand it." DeCarlos said, shaking his head up and down in agreement.

"Ok men. Time to eat. Bruce, can you lead us in prayer?" Danielle said while everyone bowed their heads.

Just then DeCarlos' phone rang. (Ring Ring) DeCarlos looked at the caller Id and saw that it was Angel, made a mental note to call her back and sent her to voicemail.

"Sorry about that," DeCarlos said to his mom and dad.

And bowed his head again. As soon as his head was down the phone rang again. He looked at the caller id and saw that it was Angel, again, Angel never calls back-to-back and then DeCarlos suddenly felt sick to his stomach. He felt that something was not right. He looked up from his phone at his parents and then excused himself from the table.

"Excuse me yall, I think this is unusually important." DeCarlos hops up from the table and walks out of the kitchen and out of the front door to answer the phone.

"Angel what's up? Everything ok?"

"No it's not, I need to talk to you. Now." She said with worry in her voice.

"Ok what's up?"

"No, not on the phone, in person. Meet me at Millwood elementary school parking lot in ten minutes. "Angel hung up without a reply.

DeCarlos still had his keys in his pocket. He darted off the porch and sped off. It took DeCarlos about 7 minutes to get to the school. He spotted Angel's Van and parked across from it. Before he could get the door opened his phone rang.

"Hey Dad"

"DeCarlos you Just going to leave in the middle of prayer"

"Sorry, it's just something is wrong right now, I don't know what it is exactly, but I will let you know when I get back"

"Ok, handle your business"

DeCarlos hopped into Angel's Van.

"Thank God you're ok!" Angel said as she hugged DeCarlos.

DeCarlos pulled back from Angel with a confused look on his face.

"What are you talking about Angel?"

"Ok look I just met with Jeff in a hotel room with three other people, we just had a meeting about making money and your name popped up, and the situation with you losing the pack. Long story short, Jeff got mad and put a key of coke on your head," Angel setback to watch the expression on DeCarlos' face.

"You mean to tell me he put a hit out on me for a brick of coke?"

"Yeah," Angel said.

DeCarlos looked at Angel then at Angel's ashtray. He noticed a half-smoked Jay, took it out and lit it. He inhaled and blew the smoke into the air, they sat in silence for a while. Then Angel spoke.

"I'm with you."

"What you talking about?"

"I know what's going on in your mind and I'm with you, whatever you need let me know and you got it."

"Ok" DeCarlos said as he nodded, looking Angel in the eyes.

"I need to know every one that was there at this meeting"

Angel nodded

"It was me, this guy named See, LJ and John, Dee acted as if he didn't want to get involved and LJ and John said they would do it gladly."

"Well I guess LJ and John will be the first ones on my list. Thanks Angel, I'll Keep in touch"

DeCarlos leaned in and gave Angel a kiss on her forehead before getting back in his car. He headed back to his house to let his dad know what happened.

Once DeCarlos got home he ran upstairs to check on Sarah. He checks the bedroom then the bathroom calls out her name as he enters each room.

"Sarah! You in here baby?"

DeCarlos gets no reply, so he walks to his parents' room and knocks on the door.

Knock, Knock, Knock

"Come on in DeCarlos" Bruce's voice rings out from the other side of the door. DeCarlos walks into the room to see his father laid across the bed, legs crossed, watching T.V.

"Dad, you know where Sarah is at?"

"Yeah, behind the curtains."

"Come on Dad I'm serious, have you seen her?"

"Yeah boy. I sent her with your mother to go stay at a friend's house for a few days. I had a feeling that shit is about to hit the fan. And based on the way you came busting in the house I think I am right?"

DeCarlos freezes at the door for a moment before answering.

"Yeah. I'm pretty sure it is."

Bruce cut off the TV and took a deep breath.

"Ok DeCarlos what was the phone call about?"

"Jeff just put a price on my head"

Bruce didn't have to say 'I told you so' it was written all over his face. Then he put on his Nike boots and stood up.

"Didn't I tell you we should have just killed that nigga. Come on we gotta get up out of here cause this is the first place they going to look for you at"

DeCarlos and Bruce walk out of the house and get into their cars.

Bruce calls DeCarlos' cell phone.

"Hello".

"Follow me. We need to go to your cousin Kenson's house around the corner."

"Right behind you."

They begin to pull out of the driveway when DeCarlos noticed

Two kids around his age come from around the back of their house with handguns in their hands and run up on his father's passenger side.

BEEEEEEEEEEEEEP, BEEEEEEEEEEEEEEEEEEEP"

DeCarlos leans on the horn to warn his dad. The kids hear the horn and one aims in DeCarlos' direction letting off five shots into DeCarlos' windshield. DeCarlos leans over into the passenger seat and covers his head as large pieces of glass rain down on him.

Bang, bang, bang, bang, bang

He can hear the other kid letting off shots into his father's car. With what sounds like a smaller gun than the one that was being shot in his direction.

PAT. PAT. PAT. PAT. PAT. PAT.

Just as quick as it started, it was over with. DeCarlos laid in the seat for a few seconds to make sure they were gone. Then he yelled to his dad.

"Dad. Dad, You all right?"

"Yeah son, what about you? You hit?" Bruce yelled back.

DeCarlos sat up in his seat and looked himself over making sure there was no blood.

"Naw, I am good." DeCarlos yelled. He got out of the car to check on his father. Glass falls to the ground as DeCarlos opens his door to get out. He runs to the driver's side of Bruce's car as Bruce struggles to crawl out of the car. DeCarlos helped him get to his feet.

"You sure you ok, Dad?"

"Yeah, never better. It's been awhile since someone tried to kill me but hey gangstas don't die they multiply, ain't that right son." Bruce said, wiping off glass shards from his shirt.

DeCarlos let out a heavy laugh.

"Yeah, I guess you're right Dad. Now, let's get out of here before these amateurs come back and try to finish the job."

"Yeah, your right son. Let's go" Bruce hopped back in his car and so did DeCarlos. They drove around the corner to Kenson's house.

Once they arrived, they pulled into the garage and closed it. Walked into the house and saw Kenson at the table eating.

"What's up cuz?" Bruce greeted Kenson.

"What up?" Kenson replied and then turned to DeCarlos.

"What's up cuz"

"What up Kenson" DeCarlos replied

"Heard you had a little problem"

"Yeah, just a little problem though, nothing too big."

"That's good to hear because if it was a big problem then it would be a lot of people coming out of retirement to help you out. You know that right?"

"Actually, no I didn't," DeCarlos said honestly while taking a seat at the table and grabbing a piece of chicken from Kenson's plate."

"You better be glad you my little cousin DeCarlos"

"What you say that for? DeCarlos asks playfully, his mouth filled with

74

chicken and looking up in the middle of a big bite as if he had done nothing wrong.

"No reason DeCarlos, you smoke? Kenson asked as he opened one of the drawers in the kitchen, pulled out some weed and began rolling a jay.

"Yeah, I smoke." he said after swallowing another huge bite of the chicken.

Bruce sat down at the table and pulled out his lighter to hand to Kenson.

"We're going to need a couple cars"

"Cool". Kenson gets the jay from Bruce and inhales and then exhales.

"Let me make a couple phone calls right quick I'll be back." Kenson said before he walked off to one of the back rooms, while he was gone Bruce and DeCarlos passed the Jay and made a game plan.

"DeCarlos, once we get these cars go by his house and see if you can catch him slipping. He just might be too smart for his own good." Bruce took a sip of the beer and grabbed the jay.

"Aight Dad. Where we gonna meet up afterwards though?"

"Imma get us a room out in the city. A lowkey spot. No one will know we are there." Bruce takes out his cell phone, makes a reservation, and then hangs up.

"Okay DeCarlos, we set. As long as we get the cars tonight, we good."

"Aight, let's do it."

At that moment Kenson comes back in the room grabs the jay and sits at the table.

"Ok, the cars are ready, they'll be here in 30 minutes. Yall need anything else?" Kenson asked, looking back and forth between DeCarlos and Bruce.

"Yeah, cousin Kenson," DeCarlos replied quickly.

"What you need lil cuz?"

"We need some more of that weed and some more chicken."

DeCarlos and Kenson broke out into laughter.

"You know what DeCarlos, I am with you on that one" Kenson said.

"Me too," Bruce chimed in.

For the next hour they sat smoking, eating, and talking shit until Kenson's phone rang.

Hello, ok, see you tomorrow" Kenson hung up the phone.

"Cars are here, they are two houses down with white towels hanging from the back window. Keys are under the floor mats."

"Thanks cousin Kenson," DeCarlos said as he got up and gave Kenson a handshake and hug.

"No problem DeCarlos. If you ever need me for anything let me know. Oh by the way there are a couple straps under the seats as well if you need them"

"Okay cuz."

"You ready to roll DeCarlos" Bruce said as he got up out of the seat and headed for the door.

"Naw Cuz, yall ain't about to leave before yall throw them bones away and put the dishes in the sink" Kenson said as he grabbed his plate and threw his bones away.

"Aight, we got you cuz" DeCarlos and Bruce both said.

After they finished cleaning off their plates they left and went to the cars. They both got in and found the keys where Kenson said they would be.

"Ok DeCarlos, you know where Van Ness Metro station is?"

"Yeah, it's right there by DCU,"

"Exactly. After you make your check come out there, I will be in room 207 at the Days Inn up the street."

"Aight see you then."

DeCarlos pulls off and heads around Jeff's house hoping to see him outside. He doesn't see him, so he parks and goes around back to look through the back window. He sees nothing and goes back to the car. He sits there for almost 2 hours with no luck. He finally pulls off and heads uptown, 45 minutes later he parks his car at the hotel and heads up to room 207.

In the Hotel room on Connecticut Avenue NW DeCarlos sits at the table breaking down his beretta nine-millimeter and cleaning it. While Bruce sits on the edge of the bed listening to the radio and rolling a Jay.

"Hey dad, I went by Jeff's house today and haven't seen his car outside at all. I even peeked in the back window at the house and there's no sign of him at all."

"It's okay son. He will pop up eventually. Dead or alive he will pop up. Have you been to school lately?"

"Dad, are you serious right now?"

Bruce lights up the jay and moves to the table so he can sit across from DeCarlos.

"I'm dead serious." Bruce said as he takes a couple of pulls from the jay and passes it to DeCarlos.

"Not with what's been going on in these streets lately." DeCarlos said before taking a few hits of the jay.

"Well you might have already found him if you did. I'm pretty sure one of your little friends knows where he's at. Why don't you reach out to a couple of them and see what you can get poppin'?"

Imma call his mom and just start some convo so I can feel her out to see what she knows."

Bruce grabbed the jay from DeCarlos and walked over to the bed and began to dial numbers on his cell phone. DeCarlos put his gun down, pulled out his cell also and dialed Dian's number. In the third ring she picked up.

"Hello"

"Hey Diane"

"Who this?"

"You don't recognize my voice yet? And we've known each other since middle school."

"I don't like guessing games. Who is this?"

DeCarlos had to smile at that one.

"This is DeCarlos. How you been?"

"Hey DeCarlos. Boy, I ain't seen or heard from you in a while. You don't come to school no more. This the first time you done called me in like months. Anyway, to answer your question I been doin good.

How are you and Sarah doing?"

DeCarlos walks over to Bruce and grabs the jay. He takes a few pulls and exhales the smoke from his lungs slowly before answering.

"I'm still alive so I can't complain. Sarah is doing well she at home taking care of our daughter.

I ain't even gonna lie, waking up at two or three in the morning is really starting to kick my ass."

Diane laughs on the other end of the phone.

"Hey but check this out, have you seen Jeff around school or heard where he might be?" DeCarlos asks as he sits back into his chair.

"Naw I haven't seen him in a while either. Everything ok?" Diane asks with a worry in her voice.

Bruce taps the table twice to get DeCarlos' attention and then gave him a thumbs up, DeCarlos nods.

"Yeah, everything's cool, it's just that he ain't picking up his cell phone and his moms been looking for him, that's all. Hey, I got another call coming in from a blocked number, it may be him let me hit you back later, ok?"

"Okay. Bye DeCarlos."

"Bye Diane"

DeCarlos hangs the phone up and looks at Bruce.

"What you got Dad?"

Bruce takes a couple of puffs then hands the jay back to DeCarlos

"The rest of that is you DeCarlos"

"Aight, that's what's up" DeCarlos said as he reaches out for the little piece of a jay that is left.

"I talked to Stephanie, and she said the little nigga at home with his little girlfriend. And he been using his girl's car to get around. That's why you haven't seen his car out front. She also told me that all they do every day is smoke and listen to music. She said she is "tired of it".

"What else she say?"

"That's it"

DeCarlos took the last few pulls of the Jay and put it out.

"Okay, well now we got to come up with a plan."

DeCarlos and Bruce sat for about five minutes thinking and then out of nowhere DeCarlos jumps up.

"I got it!"

"What's up son? Talk to me."

"Aight listen up old man. You call Stephanie back and tell her you want to take her out. Give her some lame ass story about getting out of the house and enjoying the night to forget about Jeff getting on her nerves. That will give me the time I need to get into the house and grab Jeff."

"Aight. I'll call her, but little nigga you better not ever tell your mother because she'll kill me if she finds out I went out with that chick."

Bruce gave DeCarlos a look then pulls out his phone and gets Stephanie back on the line. After about 5 minutes he hangs up.

"Almost too easy. I am gonna pick her up in an hour" Bruce said.

"Okay, Imma need a favor before you go over there to get her. "

"Grab my bookbag out of my closet and take it over to that spot I showed you a while ago and put it in the basement aight" DeCarlos said as he stretched across the bed and turned on the TV

"Aight, I got you"

"Call me when yall leave the house so I know when I can make my move."

An hour and a half later DeCarlos is laying across the hotel bed asleep. His phone vibrates, waking him up. He answers half asleep

"Hello"

"Boy, get your ass up, it's showtime. The girlfriend drives a dark gray sedan. Its parked out front and the license plate said, "Kiss Me". Bruce hangs up the phone.

DeCarlos rushes to grab his gun off the table and runs out of the door. Thirty minutes later he makes it out to the front of Jeff's house. He sees the sedan parked out front.

He walks up to the front door and reaches under the welcome mat and retrieves a spare key.

"Thanks Jeff, for being my friend for so long I couldn't have done it without you." DeCarlos said to himself out loud before entering the key into the lock to open the door. Once DeCarlos is inside he quietly closes the door and waits there. He focuses on what he can hear as his eyes adjust to the darkness. He recognizes the rap music coming from upstairs. He pulls out his gun and heads downstairs to make sure no one is down there. He goes into room after room sweeping his gun from left to right as he enters, after making sure he is alone he heads back up the steps. At the final step the top floorboard squeaks, he drops to one knee and stays very still listening for any movement over the sound of the music. A door opens at the end of the hall and a woman comes out. The smell of weed hits DeCarlos almost immediately but he stays focused. She heads to the bathroom, turns out the light and disappears behind the door. DeCarlos sits there in pitch black darkness waiting for what is to come next. Five minutes later she comes back out and shuts the door behind her. DeCarlos gets up and puts his ear to the door to listen. All he can hear is Bone Thug's "Ecstasy" playing on the other side. He gently checks the doorknob to see if it's unlocked, turns it slowly and creeps in. Jeff was there on the bed but too busy getting his dick sucked to notice DeCarlos come in. From where DeCarlos was standing all he could see was a big round ass in the air and a fat white clean-shaven pussy. Her pussy was so pink that it made DeCarlos mouth water. He composed himself once again and then slammed the door closed, as he pointed his gun at Jeff. The girl jumped up grabbing the covers.

"Don't move nigga."

"How the fuck you get in here?" Jeff asked with the look of shock still lingering on his face.

"Let's just say I have known you a long time. DeCarlos looks over at the naked woman.

"Damn you pretty as shit, you got a phat ass and a fat pussy. "

She smiled and DeCarlos could see her cheeks turning red, slightly covered by her blonde hair.

"Thank you".

"Now, when I say this, I want you to know that I mean every word, this is going to hurt me way more than it will you." DeCarlos said. He then turned his gun on the woman shooting her in the head without much hesitation. The bullet slammed into her forehead with so much impact that it knocked her body off the bed. She was still clinching the covers as she hit the floor.

DeCarlos sat on the edge of the bed with the gun aimed at Jeff's chest.

"Have you talked to your mother lately?"

Jeff sits up

"No why"

"Cause if you don't act right and give me the info, I want she's going to die" DeCarlos said with a straight face and a slight gloss in his eyes that spoke the truth.

"Bullshit. You ain't got her, you bluffing."

DeCarlos took out his phone and put it on speaker and dialed his dad's cell number.

"Hello"

"Hey Dad. I got Jeff here and you're on speaker phone okay."

"Aight"

"How's your night going"

"It's ok I got a pretty white girl out here tonight, we at the bowling alley, hold on Jon."

"Way to go Stephanie. That's your third strike tonight. I know I am having fun too. Thanks, No problem." DeCarlo's dad could be heard over the speaker.

"Hey son got to go."

"Aight Dad, enjoy"

"I will"

Jeff's face turned red

"You really going to kill my mom cuz?"

"Yep. Almost the same way you tried to have my dad killed."

"I ain't had nothing to do with that"

"Well who did?"

"Give me 24 hours and I will have an answer"

"Wrong answer and too much time" DeCarlos got up off the bed.

"Put some clothes on, we're going for a ride."

While Jeff put on some clothes DeCarlos went over to cut off the music but made sure his gun was still aimed at Jeff. He went over and sat on the bed, watching Jeff's every move. He knew Jeff had guns hidden in his room, so he didn't take his eyes off of him. After Jeff slipped on his shoes DeCarlos asked

"You claustrophobic?"

Jeff looked at DeCarlos as if he was crazy.

"What the fuck you ask me that for?"

DeCarlos walked up to Jeff and smacked him in the mouth with the side of the gun. Jeff fell hard to the floor.

"Nigga, just answer the fucking question"

Jeff reached for his lip and wiped it then looked down at his fingers to see the blood. At that moment he realized DeCarlos was not playing.

"No, I'm not," Jeff replied.

"Good"

DeCarlos put the gun to the back of Jeff's head.

"After you, my friend."

They walk down the steps and to the front door. DeCarlos tucks the gun under his shirt as they walk out into the daylight.

"Where is your car at DeCarlos?"

DeCarlos goes to his new car and pops the trunk.

"Get in and don't make me shoot you to put you in it."

"Oh, you going to kill me like you did T?"

"No, even though you tried to kill me, you still don't deserve to die like that"

DeCarlos looks Jeff in the eyes.

"Jeff, I promise I won't kill you if you get in there."

Jeff felt a little better because he knew DeCarlos kept his promises, so he got in. DeCarlos closed the trunk of the car and drove off.

CHAPTER 15

In the basement of an abandoned house in Jeff is tied down to a chair. DeCarlos walks around Jeff in complete silence every now and then smacking Jeff in the face and back of the head. DeCarlos finally stopped in front of Jeff and they both lock eyes.

"Jeff, you real smart. Too smart at times, but there is still something that I can't wrap my mind around yet," DeCarlos pauses putting his hand on Jeff's chin he looks to be in deep thought at that moment.

"Do you know what that is Jeff?" DeCarlos asks.

"You just said I was smart, but I must not be smart enough because I don't know what the fuck you are talking about"

DeCarlos giggles a bit before he continues.

"The part I don't understand is why try to kill me and my dad after I have been nothing but loyal to you?

Okay, I'll give you the benefit of the doubt, I did lose the pack. But it was only one time. And I have known you for a while. That's not like you. So it leads me to one reason. Someone either paid you to hit us or ordered you to hit us, which was it?"

"Come on DeCarlos, I known you a long time you know good and well that I don't wanna see no harm come to you cuz."

DeCarlos' voice turns colder.

"You didn't answer my question homie."

DeCarlos goes over to a small table that was set in the corner of the basement. On the table sat a book bag. DeCarlos reaches in and grabs a pair of scissors from the bag.

He walks back over to Jeff and begins to cut his shirt down the middle from the neck down.

"Hold up cuz, what you bout to do?" Jeff said as DeCarlos proceeds to peel back the shirt revealing Jeff's chest and stomach.

Just then DeCarlos' phone rings. He answers on the second ring and puts the phone on speaker, placing it on the ground.

"Hello?"

"Hey Son,"

"Hey Dad."

"Everything going ok with Jeff?"

"Yeah, everything is good. We just about to make a little mess, that's all" DeCarlos said as he walked over to the bag and pulled out a scalpel and a squeeze bottle of lemon juice. He walks back over to Jeff.

"Help, help!" Jeff screams as reality begins to sink in.

"Shut up nigga." DeCarlos screams back. DeCarlos gets on one knee getting eye level with Jeff's chest. "Hey Dad, how did your little date go with Stephanie?" he asks.

"It went great, we went out to eat and did a little fishing. Jeff, I didn't know your mother couldn't swim."

DeCarlos and Bruce broke out in laughter. As Jeff began to realize what was going on his face started to turn blood red with rage. He starts to scream

"Fuck you Mr. Bruce. Imma kill you as soon as I see you. I wish my man ain't miss. You would have been a dead mother fucker"

DeCarlos just watches on not revealing that Jeff has given him half of the information that he needs. But he still could not wait for the rest.

"DeCarlos?"

"Yea Dad"

"Cut the music up, he's a screamer. And save some for me I'll see you when I get there"

Bruce hangs up the phone, DeCarlos looks at Jeff, still red from screaming.

"I thought you didn't know what I was talking about Jeff"

Jeff spits in DeCarlos' face

"Fuck you DeCarlos, you ain't shit"

DeCarlos wipes the spit off his eye and nose. Gets up and walks over to the radio slowly. He turns it up to the max

"You a bitch DeCarlos. I made you nigga you hear me, I made you."

Jeff continued to scream.

DeCarlos kneels back down and grabs one of Jeff's nipples, making Jeff shut up instantly. He took the scalpel and cut his nipple clean off. Jeff began to jerk back and forth screaming at the top of his lungs. DeCarlos just looks on with a devilish smile on his face as he grabs the bottle of lemon juice. He squeezed the bottle squirting juice all over Jeff's chest. He makes sure Jeff's entire chest is soaked and then starts making small cuts all over his chest.

"One, two, three, four, five, six, seven, eight, nine, ten," DeCarlos said as he slashes Jeff's chest with each stroke. With each cut Jeff jerks more and more until he becomes numb to the cuts. That is when DeCarlos turned down the music and pulled up a chair as he sat in front of Jeff.

"Ok Jeff, I know you tried to kill me and my family, but the question of why you tried is still in the air. And I am going to get an answer from you, or do we have to keep this up?". DeCarlos pointed the scalpel at the cuts that cover Jeff's body.

Jeff lets out a small chuckle

"You should know I ain't gon tell you shit! You killed my mom, do what you gotta do pussy."

DeCarlos gets up and grabs the bag off the floor and walks back to the table that sists right in front of Jeff. He neatly puts the contents in a row on the table in front of him. He grabs an ice pick out of the row and plays with it tossing it from hand to hand as if it were a baseball. He begins to walk around jeff while talking

"Jeff, if you had one wish and I could grant it, what would it be?"

Jeff lifts his head his eyes following as DeCarlos continues to circle him.

"I just wish that the Devil himself would give me the strength to break out of this chair and beat you to death with my bare hands, cut your heart outta your chest and give it to your dad as a gift".

A slight smile came across DeCarlos' face.

"I figured you might have something a little more personal to wish for"

DeCarlos all of a sudden brings the Ice Pick down with full force and rams it into Jeff's upper Thigh, causing him to scream in agony.

DeCarlos rips it out and stares as the blood drips from its tip. The sight excites DeCarlos and a thirst for more blood washes over him. He rears back and plunges the pick down again this time into Jeff's other thigh. This time he leaves it in until Jeff composes himself and stops screaming only to have DeCarlos rip it out sending another surge of pain through Jeff's entire body. He watches the blood on the pick as it slowly trickles down to form a droplet before hitting the floor and snapping DeCarlos out of his daze. DeCarlos begins to slowly walk around Jeff.

"What if I can deliver your mother to you. Alive of course, will you give me the info I need"

"Fuck you DeCarlos, Stop playing with my emotions and just kill me already"

Jeff said, gasping for air as he struggles with the pain.

"Maybe I can help you change your mind," DeCarlos said, then walks over to the tools on the floor and grabs an electric hand saw. He taps the trigger a couple times to make sure it works (zoom, zoom, zoom) the sound makes Jeff jump.

Jeff's eyes grow wider. DeCarlos notices the fear.

"Don't worry Jeff, I won't hurt you" he takes hold of the bottom of Jeff's pants leg and begins to cut it all the way up to the waist and then again on the other leg. When he was done, he took off the loose fabric exposing Jeff's dick and bare legs. DeCarlos brings the saw closer to Jeff's dick and taps the trigger as he did earlier (zoom, zoom, zoom) it was so close Jeff could feel the heat from the saw blow on him. DeCarlos watches closely at how Jeff's body tenses up which puts a smile on his face. He put the saw down on the floor and began to unlace Jeff's shoes and take them off Jeff was now fully exposed in the chair. DeCarlos reached down and grabbed a chisel and a hammer then held them up for Jeff to see.

"Since you have been trying to take stuff from me, I think it's time I get a little something from you" DeCarlos said in a cold voice. He got up and grabbed the radio and brought it over and set it next to the chair. He turned it up to the max once again. DeCarlos gets down on one knee in front of Jeff with the hammer in one hand and the chisel in the other, placing the chisel on the bone of Jeff's big toe.

He raises the hammer above his head and comes down on the chisel with so much force that it separates Jeff's big toe from his foot with one swing. Jeff's toe rolls under his chair as blood squirts out of Jeff's foot. Jeff begins to scream as he jerks from side to side trying to jump out of the chair. He only manages to knock the chair over bringing him to the floor.

"Come on now Jeff. It was only a toe stop acting like a baby who just lost his bottle" DeCarlos said as he picks up Jeff in his chair. The music continues to play, drowning out the sound of Jeff's screams. When he stops, DeCarlos turns it off.

"Jeff how about you stop making this hard for yourself and tell me who ordered the hit."

"It was Dom" Jeff whispers

I can't hear you, speak louder"

DeCarlos replied as he leans in and steps on Jeff's newly injured foot.

Jeff howls in pain once more.

"Fuck you, DeCarlos"

At that moment DeCarlos' phone rings.

"Hello"

"He talk yet?" Bruce asks.

I thought he said something, but I guess I was wrong. Won't be too much longer"

"Well I'm out front and I have someone with me he might want to meet. See you in a few"

DeCarlos hung up the phone and sat back down in the chair.

"There's someone about to come in here that I want you to see"

"There ain't nobody I want to meet just kill me already, damn"

"You never know until you see their face"

In walks Stephanie and Bruce. Bruce has a gun to Stephanie's head. Stephanie looks at DeCarlos sitting there and then over at her son. She runs over and grabs his head and starts to cry.

"Jeff, are you ok? Stephanie tries to speak as she starts sobbing uncontrollably.

"Yeah Ma, I'm maintaining"

Bruce walks over and snatches Stephanie up off Jeff and points the gun back at her head.

"Ok, playtime is over either you give us the name and address of the people who put you up to this or her brains are going to be on the floor with you watching?" Bruce said.

"Ok, ok Dom gave me the order. His address is in my phone under boss" Jeff said quickly.

"Have you been there before" DeCarlos asked.

"Yes."

"Ok you know how this goes tell me everything you know"

"He stays in this big ass Mansion with guards on patrol twenty-four seven it's only four of them but they're good."

"Ok where is the safe located?" DeCarlos asked

"It's upstairs in the last room on the left. I only saw it once and that was by accident. He also has a panic room where no one can get in or out, that's in the same room. Don't know if it's operational or not but I just seen the plans on his desk. That's all I know. Please, let my mom go."

DeCarlos looked at Bruce and they nodded slightly in silent agreement, "Ok Stephanie, you and Jeff can go. Go get your son." Bruce said as he gave Stephanie a little nudge letting her know it was ok to get Jeff.

Stephanie runs over to Jeff and unties his restraints and helps him up off the chair, raises her head and locks eyes with Bruce.

"Thank you Bruce,"

Bruce slowly lifts up his .357 and shot Stephanie and Jeff in the head as both of their bodies tumbled over the chair before hitting the ground.

"Get your toys and let's go. We got work to do" Bruce said.

to DeCarlos and then turned around and left.

Outside the abandoned house Bruce and DeCarlos get in the car and drive around the corner. They line up driver's side to driver's side.

"Hey Dad, Imma go back over Jeff house to find the phone"

"Aight Imma follow you. You never know if Dom knows this nigga missed. He might send someone over to kill him. I need to watch your back."

"Aight let's go then."

Bruce and DeCarlos drive off to Jeff's house.

Once at Jeff's house DeCarlos gets out, opens the front door and goes straight to the room. When he opens the door the smell of death hits him hard. He grabs his shirt and puts it over his nose to block the smell. He stands there and scans the room to see if he can spot the phone from where he is standing.

And to his luck, he does, right next to the radio. He runs over, grabs it and heads out the room, closes the door and takes a deep breath before going through the contacts on the phone. He goes straight to the 'p's and the first one is Plug. He taps the screen, and the contact info appears. He puts the phone in his pocket, runs out of the house and gets in the car, then looks over at Bruce.

"Dad we may need cousin Kenson again"

"Well let's go. I know he home, he's off work today"

They both pull off and drive to Kenson's house. They walk in through the garage entrance and see him in the same spot as last time.

"What up cuz. What brings you back so soon?" Kenson looks from DeCarlos to Bruce as they sit down

"Go ahead DeCarlos, tell him what's up" DeCarlos leans in.

"Ok check this out, we know who tried to kill us for real, well who was behind it at least. So Imma get straight to the point. We need some guns."

"Is it just you two or is it more"

"Just us two and we going when the sun goes down"

Kenson gets up and walks in the back room. He comes back with a duffle bag. He puts the duffle bag on the floor and walks back over to DeCarlos and Bruce.

"Everything you need is in that duffle bag by the door. I never got a chance to use those so take good care of them. And don't open it till you leave here, Got it."

"Yeah," DeCarlos said.

"Well we still have about an hour before the sun goes down. Y'all tryna smoke and play call of duty?"

DeCarlos and Bruce look at each other and in unison say

"Ok."

So, for the next two hours they play videogames and smoke. When the weed is gone DeCarlos and Bruce head to the door.

"Time to go Cuz" said Bruce to Kenson

"Stay safe yall." Kenson gave Bruce and DeCarlos a hug. DeCarlos grabs the duffle bag and heads to the car.

"Dad, follow me, I know where the place is. We can get strapped up once we get there,"

"Aight it's your show. Let's go do it."

They both get in the car and pull off.

DeCarlos and Bruce lay in the bushes that surround the front yard of Dom's home wearing all black with north face ski masks and Timberland boots. Their eyes sweep back and forth across the yard and roof of the house.

DeCarlos looks over at Bruce and said in a low voice:

"Dad, do you see the camera in the upper right corner of the front door?"

Bruce's eyes immediately shoot over to the front door as he sees the all-black camera. In the pitch-black darkness it blends in.

"Damn Boy, you got good eyes, I almost didn't see it at all. In my defense, I'm getting old."

"Yeah, I know old man" DeCarlos said with a smile while still looking at the front of the house.

DeCarlos notices movement on the roof.

"Dad, I hope your shot is as good as it used to be."

Bruce pulls up his AK-47 with scope and suppressor and makes sure DeCarlos can see it.

"Boy, I'll never lose the ability to be an efficient killer."

"Good, because this bitch nigga got guards on the roof. Do you see the two guards with the M16's walking back and forth?"

"Yeah, I see them but there not going to be too much of a problem" Bruce lifts up the AK and looks through the scope. He puts one of the guards in his crosshairs. He breathes deep so he can hear his heartbeat. He holds his breath waiting for the right moment to pull the trigger.

"Dad hold up, hold up" DeCarlos said as he taps Bruce's arm.

Bruce turns and gave him an annoyed look

"What boy! I was just about to take the shot ``Bruce snapped at him in a whisper.

"Look, look." He said while pointing his AR-15 with infrared laser and suppressor towards the figures coming out of the front door. It was Dom and two of his bodyguards dressed in red suits with white shirts and shoes.

"Let's make this easy shall we. You take out the two bodyguards and I will take out the ones on the roof on the count of three.

"One." Bruce said as he put one of the guards on the roof in his sights.

"Two."

The bodyguards and Dom were walking straight towards them. DeCarlos put the laser on the biggest bodyguard's head and waited

"Three."

Bruce whispered as he squeezed the trigger and killed one on the roof then quickly took out the rest as DeCarlos did the same with one shot to the head of each of the bodyguards.

Before the second body hit the ground Dom took off running back towards the front door.

DeCarlos stood up and put the laser on the back of Dom's head but right before he got a chance to shoot Bruce grabbed his ankle.

"Hold up son. Let him get inside before you shoot him in the leg."

Bruce took off running towards the front door. Bruce watched as Dom scrambled for his keys. He kept looking back at Bruce while he ran full speed. Dom dropped the keys which gave Bruce a few extra seconds to get closer. Dom picked up his keys and opened the front door but before he was able to step inside, he fell to the ground as a bullet from DeCarlos gun slammed into the back of his leg and came out of the front shattering every bit of bone and cartilage that was in its path. Not a second later Bruce is on top of Dom, his hand covering his mouth to muffle his screams.

Shut up bitch, it's only a flesh wound" Bruce lied to him to get him to calm down, but it didn't work. He moved around squirming to get Bruce's hand off his

mouth. Bruce took out his .357 snub nose and hit Dom, striking him on the right side of the temple putting him out cold. He grabs Dom off the floor and slings him over his shoulder. Just then DeCarlos ran in, shutting the door behind him.

"Dad, what the fuck are you doing?"

"What! I had to knock the bitch nigga out cause he was moving too much." Bruce explained while walking up the steps towards the room with the safe.

Once in the room, DeCarlos rips out the phone cords and ties Dom's legs and hands. He goes and gets a bowl of water. He sets it on the table then turns to Bruce.

"Ok, Dad where do we go from here?"

"Sit him up and put him in the chair over there in the corner".

DeCarlos does as he is asked, propping Dom up into the chair.

"Ok, now throw that water in his face to wake him up."

DeCarlos grabs the bowl and throws the water in Dom's face. Almost immediately Dom wakes up.

"What the fuck" Dom yells. and then looks at the two masked men that stood in front of him.

"We want the money nothing else. We don't want the drugs or your life, but if you force us to take it, we will." Bruce said and paused to make sure the words were understood.

You have not seen our faces yet, and hopefully, we won't have to ask where the money is?" DeCarlos said.

"Do you know who the fuck I am, you stupid mother fuckers" Dom yelled, his anger rising. DeCarlos looked around the room and noticed a radio in the corner. He cut it on and turned the music up loud. To his surprise, classical music was playing. DeCarlos took out his Glock nine and walked over to Dom. His eyes began to open wide because he knew he was going to die. He starts pleading for his life.

"No. Please don't kill me. I'll give you whatever you want" Dom tries to plead with them.

Unphased DeCarlos puts the gun to Dom's temple looking him straight in the eyes.

DeCarlos moves the gun slowly to Dom's forehead never losing eye contact. This made Dom even more scared. He began to cry and scream as he struggled to get up.

"No, No. Please don't do it."

His screams couldn't be heard over the music, so it had no effect on DeCarlos. As soon as he tried to get up, DeCarlos shot him in the knee, and he crashed to the floor in pain. DeCarlos picked him up and put him back in the chair. This time he tied him to the seat. Bruce went over and cut the radio off, he leaned against the table and glancing over at Dom while shaking his head.

"Why you making us do this to you Dom. It doesn't have to be this way; all we want is the money."

"Ok, ok, ok. Go over there behind the desk and look under the arm of the chair and push the button. Just please stop shooting me!"

Bruce ran over to the big wooden office desk, pulled out the black leather chair on wheels and found the button under the right side of the armrest and pushed it.

The wall behind him swung open and a 10-foot safe appeared.

"Ok, what's the combo?"

"It's thirty-thirty three- three,"

"Nigga, really…" Bruce said in disbelief.

Dom said from the chair, blood starting to pool around his feet.

Bruce put in the combination and opened the safe. What he saw inside was far greater than he had ever imagined. There were about thirty neatly packed bricks of cocaine.

That lined the top of the safe then there was stacks of money that came up to about three feet high. The smell of all that fresh money was the best fragrance in the world to them.

"DeCarlos come look at this!" DeCarlos walked over to the safe and his mouth dropped. All he could think about was Sarah and how happy she would be.

"DeCarlos, DeCarlos!" Dom shouted as he began to realize who the masked man was.

"DeCarlos, Imma kill you. You son of a bitch you're a dead man" he continued to shout.

DeCarlos took his mask off and put it in his pocket then, without a word he walked over and punched Dom in his mouth.

"Dom, why you have to talk to my son like that?" Bruce said then takes his mask off as well.

"Br-Br Bruce is that you? It can't be. You're dead!" Dom screamed.

DeCarlos pointed his gun at Dom's head.

"Fuck that nigga, we'll kill him when we get all of this money, come help me find out what to put all this money in," Bruce said to DeCarlos. Then he turned to Dom, "How much is it?"

"Five-hundred grand" he answered reluctantly.

"OK." DeCarlos and Bruce rush out of the room and find a row of empty army duffle bags when all of a sudden, they hear a crash come out of the room where Dom was. They rush to the room guns drawn and watch as Dom crawls towards a panic room.

DeCarlos lets off two shots. They hit Dom in the back, and he screams and suddenly he is unable to move. Bruce and DeCarlos slowly approach Dom, his eyes wide with panic. They turn him over. He tries to yell but no sound comes out. He cannot move and the reality sets in, he realizes he is paralyzed, trying to mouth the word no as Bruce and DeCarlos raise their weapons to point directly at Dom's face. They unload 10 shots each.

Bang, Bang, Bang, Bang, Bang, Bang, Bang, Bang, Bang, Bang

"Ok DeCarlos, let's pack all this stuff up and let's go." Bruce said. DeCarlos and Bruce grab the duffle bags and begin to fill them up. Once everything is out of the safe, they grab the bags and run out the front door. In the distance, the sounds of police sirens could be heard and with the sounds of sirens getting closer and closer. They can see the lights bouncing off the trees.

DeCarlos screams. "We have to get to the car, hurry!"

END

ABOUT THE AUTHOR

From an early age Twizz knew he wanted more out of life. Falling in with a dangerous crowd and wanting to make a name for himself he ended up making some mistakes along the way. Now, he hopes to use his experiences and stories to help others to choose a better path.

Made in the USA
Columbia, SC
07 January 2023

74454914R00054